Alarm Bells Wen

Having a nice, mutuall one thing. Actually get involved was something else again...

Davis had never spent so much time thinking about a woman he hardly knew. Whether it was Marie's big green eyes or the adrenaline rush her driving had given him, something about her had hit him hard.

He much preferred a simple, no-ties-involved relationship. And Marie Santini was practically encircled by a white picket fence. Everything about her screamed out hearth and home. Altogether a dangerous female.

But then, marines were supposed to thrive on danger, right?

Dear Reader

Merry Christmas! We have six seasonal treats just for you in Desire this month.

Popular author Cait London gives us MAN OF THE MONTH, Tyrell Blaylock in *Typical Male*. He's another one of her Blaylock men; when they set their sights on something—or *someone*—there's no stopping them! Cait's back with another MAN OF THE MONTH in February 2001.

THE MILLIONAIRE'S CLUB concludes this month with Cindy Gerard's *Lone Star Prince*—where hero Greg Stone recognises the features of Princess Anna's four-year-old son as being remarkably like his own! We also begin a new trilogy by Elizabeth Bevarly, on a theme she's used before—FROM HERE TO MATERNITY. Look out for the next two titles in February and April 2001.

Maureen Child's back with another hunky Marine in *Marine Under the Mistletoe*. And there's a very special little person being delivered by Christmas in Christy Lockhart's *The Cowboy's Christmas Baby*. Finally, don't miss a classic fairy-tale-come-true in Kathryn Jensen's *I Married A Prince*.

Enjoy,

The Editors

Marine under
the Mistletoe

MAUREEN CHILD

™ SILHOUETTE
DESIRE®

DID YOU PURCHASE THIS BOOK WITHOUT A COVER?

If you did, you should be aware it is **stolen property** as it was reported *unsold and destroyed* by a retailer. Neither the author nor the publisher has received any payment for this book.

All the characters in this book have no existence outside the imagination of the author, and have no relation whatsoever to anyone bearing the same name or names. They are not even distantly inspired by any individual known or unknown to the author, and all the incidents are pure invention.

All Rights Reserved including the right of reproduction in whole or in part in any form. This edition is published by arrangement with Harlequin Enterprises II B.V. The text of this publication or any part thereof may not be reproduced or transmitted in any form or by any means, electronic or mechanical, including photocopying, recording, storage in an information retrieval system, or otherwise, without the written permission of the publisher.

This book is sold subject to the condition that it shall not, by way of trade or otherwise, be lent, resold, hired out or otherwise circulated without the prior consent of the publisher in any form of binding or cover other than that in which it is published and without a similar condition including this condition being imposed on the subsequent purchaser.

Silhouette, Silhouette Desire and Colophon are registered trademarks of Harlequin Books S.A., used under licence.

First published in Great Britain 2000
Silhouette Books, Eton House, 18-24 Paradise Road, Richmond, Surrey TW9 1SR

© Maureen Child 1999

ISBN 0 373 76258 5

22-1200

Printed and bound in Spain
by Litografía Rosés S.A., Barcelona

MAUREEN CHILD

was born and raised in Southern California, and is the only person she knows who longs for an occasional change of season. She is delighted to be writing for Silhouette® and is especially excited to be a part of the Desire™ line.

An avid reader, Maureen looks forward to those rare rainy California days when she can curl up and sink into a good book. Or two. When she isn't busy writing, she and her husband of twenty-five years like to travel, leaving their two grown-up children in charge of the neurotic golden retriever who is the *real* head of the household. Maureen is also an award-winning author under the names Kathleen Kane and Ann Carberry.

Maureen Child on...

The ultimate romantic meal:
'Any kind of chocolate.'

Keeping love alive in a relationship:
'Laughter.'

The quality she most admires in a man:
'A sense of humour.'

The most romantic place she's ever travelled:
'Ireland.'

One

She recognized his attitude.

Marie Santini stared out through the front windows of her auto repair shop at the man standing in her driveway. It wasn't easy to get a good look at him, what with the holly and snowmen painted on the window glass, but she gave it a try. Tall, she thought, dark hair, cut short, aviator-style sunglasses even though the day was too cloudy to make them necessary, and a hard, strong jaw with a stubborn chin.

Perfect.

Just what she needed. Another male with a protective streak toward his car. Honestly. A woman's car broke down, she brought it into the shop and picked it up when it was ready. A *man* hovered over the blasted thing like it was a woman in labor, questioning everything Marie did to his baby and winced with sympathy pains.

Now, Marie Santini liked cars as much as anybody else, but she knew for a fact that they didn't bleed when operated on. Still, she told herself, business had been slow in the last week. Maybe she'd better just step outside and coax Mr. Nervous into the shop. She grabbed her navy blue sweatshirt, tugged it on and left it unzipped to display the slogan on her red T-shirt that read Marie Santini, Car Surgeon. Then she headed for the door.

"This is a *garage?"*

Davis Garvey stared at the small but tidy auto repair shop. Wide plank walls were painted a brilliant white, the window trim and the cozy-looking shutters were an electric blue and some kind of purple and white flowers blossomed enthusiastically in terra-cotta planters on either side of the front door. Off to the side, a garage bay stood, its double doors open to reveal what looked like a mile of Peg-Board on which hundreds of obviously well-cared-for tools hung from hooks and glittered in the overhead lights.

Except for the garage bay, the place looked more like a trendy little tea shop than anything else.

He'd expected something bigger. Showier, somehow. The way the marines at Camp Pendleton talked about this shop, he had thought the place would reek of money and experience. Yet the proof that he was in the right place was emblazoned across the front of the little building. A boldly painted sign in red, white and blue proclaimed Santini's.

He frowned, remembering the guys who had told him about this place. Their voices hushed almost reverently, they'd told him, "If Marie Santini can't fix your car, nobody can."

Still, Davis thought, the idea of a woman working on his car was a hard one to swallow. But with things at Camp Pendleton as busy as they were, he had no time to do the job himself.

A cold winter wind whistled off the nearby ocean, and he jammed his hands into the pockets of his faded, worn Levi's. Tipping his head back, he watched gray clouds bunching and gathering above and wondered what had happened to the sunny California he'd always heard about. Heck, he'd been at Pendleton a week and it had either rained or threatened to rain some more.

Then a door opened and Davis snapped his attention to the front of the shop and the woman just stepping outside. He watched her as she walked toward him. She had black, shoulder-length hair, tucked behind her ears to show off small silver hoops in her lobes, and she wore a red T-shirt tucked into worn jeans, tennis shoes and a dark blue zippered sweatshirt that flapped like wings in the wind. Taller than she looked at a distance, the top of her head hit him about at chin level when she stopped directly in front of him.

"Hi," she said, and gave him a warm smile that took away some of the afternoon chill.

"Hi," he said, and looked down into the greenest

eyes he'd ever seen. Okay, he didn't know if Marie Santini knew anything about cars. But hiring this woman to welcome customers was definitely a good business move. Not pretty exactly, but she had the kind of face that made a person look twice. It was more than appearance. It was something shining in her eyes, something...*alive*.

A second or two passed before she asked, "Can I help you?"

Davis blinked and reminded himself why he was there. To find out if the "Miracle Worker" the guys had told him about was worthy to work on his car. And he couldn't do that until he actually met Marie Santini. He could always get to know the welcoming committee later.

"I don't think so," he said. "I'd like to see Marie Santini."

She blew out a breath that ruffled a few stray wisps of black hair, then said, "You're looking at her."

No way. "You?" he asked, letting his gaze rake her up and down, noting her slender build. "You're a mechanic?"

She shook her hair back from her face when the wind tossed it across her eyes. "Around here," she told him, "I'm *the* mechanic."

"You're Marie Santini?" When the guys had told him about a female mechanic, somehow he'd imagined a woman more along the lines of a German opera singer. Brunhilde.

She glanced down, unzipped her sweatshirt a bit

wider, then looked up at him again. "That's what my shirt says."

"You don't look the part," he said, and wondered just how good she could be if she didn't even have grease under her fingernails. What did she do? Wear elbow-length white gloves for oil changes?

"You were expecting maybe Two-Ton Tessie covered in axle grease?" She folded her arms across her chest, and Davis told himself not to notice the curve of her breasts. For Pete's sake, he was interviewing a mechanic. Breasts shouldn't come into this at all!

"Sorry to shatter your expectations," she said, "but I'm a darn good mechanic."

"You sound pretty sure of yourself."

"I ought to be," she muttered. "I spend half my time proving myself to men just like you."

"What do you mean, men like me?"

"Men who assume a woman can't know more about cars than a man."

"Hey, wait a minute," he said, folding his arms over his chest and glaring down at her. Nobody called him a chauvinist and got away with it. Hell, he worked with women every day on base. Darn good marines, too, all of them. He didn't necessarily have a problem with a woman mechanic. He had a problem with *any* mechanic working on his cars. Hell, if he wasn't so busy at the base right now, he'd have fixed the car himself and never have met Marie.

"No," she interrupted, "*you* wait a minute." She shook her head and threw her hands high. "You came to me. I didn't hunt you down and demand to work on your car."

"Yeah," he said.

"So have you changed your mind?"

"I don't know yet."

"Well," she said, "why don't we find out?" She started past him toward the Mustang he'd left parked at the curb.

He was only a step or two behind her. "Are you this charming to all of your customers?"

"Only the stubborn ones," she told him over her shoulder.

"I'm surprised you're still in business," he muttered, deliberately keeping his gaze from locking on to the sway of her behind.

"You won't be once I've fixed your car."

If he didn't know better, he'd swear she was a marine.

Marie didn't even want to think about how many times she'd been through this conversation. Since taking over her father's auto shop two years ago, every new customer who'd entered the place had given her the same look of disbelief.

It had stopped being amusing a long time ago.

So why, she wondered, was she enjoying herself now?

She stopped alongside his Mustang and glanced up into his big blue eyes. An utterly feminine reaction swelled in the pit of her stomach and she tamped it down fast. Honestly, she'd seen broad shoulders and strong jaws before. Silently she re-

minded herself that he was here to see her as a mechanic—not a woman. Hardly a rarity. "Let me
guess. You've never seen a woman mechanic before."

"Not lately," he admitted.

She had to give him credit. He was recovering
from his surprise a lot more quickly than most of
her customers. But then, she thought, *he* was a lot
more...*everything* than most men. Broader shoulders, more muscular build, longer legs, a square,
firm jaw, and those sharp blue eyes of his looked as
though he could see right through her.

Which, she told herself with an inward sigh, most
men did.

She'd learned years ago that men didn't see their
mechanic as possible date material. Poker buddy,
sure. A Dear Abby to the lovelorn, great. But a *real*
woman? Prospective wife and mother-type female?
No way.

"A first time for everything, Sergeant," she said.

His eyebrows shot up and Marie just managed to
swallow a smile at his surprise.

"How'd you know I'm a sergeant?" he asked.

Not a difficult call for someone who'd grown up
in Bayside. With Camp Pendleton less than a mile
or so up the road, the little town was usually crawling with marines. They were easy enough to spot,
even in civilian clothes.

"It's not hard," she said, enjoying his surprise.
"Regulation haircut—" she paused and indicated
his stance pointedly "plus you're standing like
someone just shouted, 'At ease.'"

He frowned to himself, noting his feet braced wide apart and his hands locked behind his back. Deliberately he shifted position.

"Then," she went on, smiling, "as to your rank... You're too old to be a private, too ambitious or proud looking to still be a corporal and you don't appear nearly arrogant enough to be an officer. Therefore," she finished with a half bow, "sergeant."

Impressed and amused in spite of himself, Davis nodded. "First sergeant, actually."

"I stand corrected." Marie looked into those blue eyes of his and saw what she briefly thought might be interest. No. Probably just instinctive, she told herself. A man like him was no doubt accustomed to flirting with women. *All* women. "So," she said, getting a mental grip of her hormones, "what's the problem?"

"You're the mechanic," he challenged. "You tell me."

A spurt of irritation rushed through her. She should be used to this. He wasn't the first, nor would he be the last man to test her knowledge of cars before entrusting his "baby" to her care. Although, she admitted with pride, once she'd fixed a car, it stayed fixed. And her customer base was a loyal one.

"Why is it, do you think," she asked him, "that men can design dresses for a living and be respected while a woman mechanic has to do tricks to prove herself?" He opened his mouth to speak, but she went on instead. "Do you think anybody makes Calvin Klein thread a needle himself before hiring him?''

He shook his head. ''No. But then if ol' Calvin sews a crooked hem, the dress doesn't blow up, does it?''

Okay, maybe he had a point.

''All right,'' she said, surrendering to the inevitable, ''let's take it for a test drive, shall we? Keys?'' She held out her hand and Davis looked at it for a long moment before lifting his gaze to hers.

''How about I drive?'' he asked.

''Not a chance.'' She shook her head and gave him a sympathetic glance, but didn't budge otherwise. ''I have to drive it to get the feel of it,'' she said. Then she pointed out, ''besides, you'll have to trust me with it eventually.''

That smile on her face was confident and entirely too attractive. To stifle that thought and any that might follow. Davis dropped his keys into her outstretched palm. Sliding into the passenger seat, he watched her buckle up, then turn the key in the ignition. The Mustang rumbled into life.

He glanced over his shoulder at the still-open auto shop. ''Aren't you going to—?''

''Shh,'' she told him with a frown.

He was so surprised, he did. It had been a long time since anyone had told him to shut up.

Cocking her head toward the engine, she closed her eyes and listened with all of the concentrated effort of a doctor holding a stethoscope over her patient's chest.

A moment later, she opened her eyes, sat back

and shoved the car into gear. "What were you saying?"

"Don't you want to lock your shop?"

"Won't be gone that long," she told him with a grin. Then she glanced over her left shoulder, stepped on the gas and pulled away from the curb with enough speed to launch them into space.

Davis fell back in his seat as Marie drove like she was in the lead car at the Indianapolis 500.

The beach town's narrow streets were crowded with shoppers and bedecked with holiday garlands and plastic candy canes. He winced as she threaded her way expertly in and out of traffic. She squeezed past a city bus with less than a single coat of paint to spare, then turned down an even narrower, one-way street.

A couple of people waved to her as she passed and she smiled a greeting, never really taking her eyes off the road. She worked the clutch, brake and gas pedals like a concert pianist, and Davis found himself staring at her long legs as her feet moved and danced across the car's floor.

With the convertible top down, ocean air whipped around them, sending Marie's hair into a wild, shining black tangle. It was the first time he'd ridden in a convertible with a woman who wasn't moaning about the state of her hairdo and pleading with him to raise the top.

She took the next corner practically on two wheels and darted between a surfboard-laden station wagon and an ancient Lincoln. Ahead, the signal turned from green to red without benefit of yellow and she slammed on the brakes. He jerked forward in his seat, thanked the Fates for seat belts and ground his teeth together.

Glancing at him, she said, "It's got a flat spot."

"What?" he asked, trying to unlock his jaw.

"The engine," she told him. "A flat spot when you step on the gas. It pauses, then catches."

"You're right," he acknowledged, and rubbed the whiplash feeling out of the back of his neck. "But how you even noticed a pause while driving at light speed is beyond me."

She laughed, and damned if he didn't enjoy the sound of it.

Before he could say so, though, the light turned green and she was off again.

People, cars and scenery became a colorful blur. Davis's grip on the armrest tightened until he thought he'd snap the vinyl-covered shelf clean off.

A few seconds later, she was parking the car in her driveway, shutting off the engine and giving the dashboard a loving pat. "Nice car," she said.

He inhaled slowly, deeply, grateful to have survived. Hell, he'd been in combat zones and felt more optimistic about living through the day.

Now that their mad rush through traffic was over, he turned his head and gaped at her. "You drive like a maniac."

She grinned, clearly unoffended. "That's what my dad used to say."

"Smart man," Davis managed to grind out. "How about I deal with him, instead?"

She sobered quickly. "I wish you could. But he passed away two years ago."

"Oh. Sorry." He heard the echo of pain in her voice and knew that she still missed him.

"You couldn't have known," Marie told him. "So," she added, "do you want me to fix this baby for you or not?"

Spotting a problem and knowing how to fix it were two different things. Besides, if her car-repair skills were as reckless as her driving, he could be asking for trouble here. "How do I know you *can* fix it?"

She leaned one forearm across the top of the steering wheel and shifted in her seat, turning to face him. "I guess you don't, Sergeant. You'll just have to take a chance."

"I just took enough chances for a lifetime."

Her grin widened. "I thought you marines liked a little risk now and then."

"Lady, I'm just glad you don't drive a tank."

"Me, too," she said, then added, "though I'd like to give it a try someday."

Davis laughed shortly. "I bet you would."

If he wasn't careful, he could get to like this woman. She was damned unusual, though. No open flirting. No coy smiles. Just confidence and a take-no-prisoners attitude. She had a great laugh, amazing eyes and a figure that would be able to thaw the polar ice caps. Damn, if he wasn't responding to her in a big way.

"So? Are you going to trust me with your baby?"

A challenge gleamed in her eyes and he automatically responded to it. But what marine wouldn't?

"Okay, Car Surgeon," he said, "you're on."

She nodded. "Come on into the shop, I'll write it up."

He watched her as she climbed out of the Mustang, cheeks flushed, eyes bright, her long, lean limbs carrying her in an easy stride toward the office. And Davis knew he'd never think of mechanics in the same way again.

Two

Marie felt his gaze on her as surely as she would have his touch. At *that* thought, a small shiver of anticipation rattled along her spine even as the still-rational corner of her mind told her to forget it.

Guys like him were never interested in women like her.

Behind her, she heard his car door open, then close. The soft crunch of his footsteps on the gravel drive heralded his approach. Her mouth went dry. Ridiculous. She was way too old to get butterflies just because some man gave her a second look. Some *gorgeous* man, she silently corrected. She stepped behind the counter, picked up a pen and started filling out the work order.

He walked into the office and stopped directly opposite her.

"So," she asked, with what she hoped was a professionally casual tone, "I need your name and address and a phone number where you can be reached."

He nodded and took the pen from her, his fingers brushing hers lightly in the process. Her skin tingled and she shrugged it off as static electricity. The fact that no one else had ever given her a spark like that in the office was beside the point. As he filled in the form, he asked, "How long is this going to take? I need my car."

Ah, she thought, there was definitely safety in sticking to business.

"Everybody does," she pointed out. "But I'm pretty open right now. Shouldn't take more than a couple of days."

He glanced at her. "You do all the work yourself?"

Was he still hoping there'd be a man overseeing her work? A bit defensive, she said, "Yes, it's just me. Well, except for Tommy Doyle who comes in three afternoons a week. Does that worry you?"

"That depends. Who's Tommy Doyle, and is he going to be working on my car?"

"Tommy's sixteen, and no, he's not." She waved one hand at the open doorway leading into the service bay. "He cleans up and gives me a hand sometimes."

His expression clearly said, "Keep that kid away from my car."

"Look, Sergeant—"

"Call me Davis."

Oh, she didn't think so. No point in getting on a first-name basis with the man. Better she keep this professional. As she knew it would stay. He might give her behind and her legs the once-over, but when it came right down to it, men just weren't interested in dating their mechanic.

"*Sergeant,* I can fix your car. If you want to leave it here, I can give you a loaner for a couple of days."

His eyebrows lifted. "A loaner?"

"Yeah," she said, knowing he was thinking that a business as small as hers wouldn't have anything so civilized as loaner cars. But she had a few. Of course, they didn't look like much, since she tended to buy old junkers and get them into running condition for just such situations. "You can take the Bug out there."

He glanced over his shoulder at the battered gray-and-red Volkswagen. Dents dotted its surface and splotches of primer paint made it look as though it had a skin condition.

She noted his expression and fought down a smile. "It's not a beauty," she admitted, "but it will get you back and forth to the base."

"Will it get me to a restaurant, too?" he asked, sliding his gaze back to her.

"Wherever you aim it, it will go," she assured him. "Though the valets at the Five Crowns might not want to park it for you."

Just the thought of her poor little Bug cruising up the elegant drive of the best restaurant on the coast brought a smile to her face. That smile faded when he spoke again.

"I was thinking more along the lines of that coffee shop I passed on my way here—if I could buy you some lunch."

Her stomach skittered nervously and she didn't like it. She much preferred being in control. And as long as she was being Marie the mechanic, she was. But heck, nobody ever asked her out. Men didn't usually look past her skills with tools to search for the woman within.

And now that it had happened, she wasn't real sure how to respond. So she settled for what felt natural—making a joke.

"At three o'clock in the afternoon?" She forced a laugh she didn't feel to let him know she wasn't taking him seriously and so he shouldn't worry about a thing. "A little late for lunch."

"And early for dinner," he agreed. "But they'd probably serve us anyway."

"Uh...thanks," she said, shaking her head and taking the completed form from him. "But I've got work to do and besides, I don't date—"

"Marines?" he finished for her.

"Customers," she corrected, though if she wanted to, she could have told him her sentence had been pretty much complete the first time. She didn't date. Period. In fact, Marie couldn't remember the last time she'd had a real date.

No. Wait a minute. That was wrong. She could remember. She'd just made a conscious effort to forget the experience. As any sane woman would.

Two years ago it was, just before Papa died. And the night had ended early as soon as her date blew a tire. He didn't know how to fix the flat and had wanted to call the auto club. But since they were already late for the movie, Marie had fixed it herself.

Judging from her date's expression as he rolled past her house fifteen minutes later and practically shoved her out the door, she'd committed a sin the equivalent of a girl beating up the bully picking on her boyfriend.

"Well, then," he said with another of those slow smiles, "we'll just have to wait until my car is officially off your lot and I'm no longer a customer."

Where was all this coming from? she wondered. On the test drive, he'd looked like he wanted to strangle her. Now he's all smiles and invites? Why?

And why did that gleam in his eyes make her as nervous as she'd been the first time she'd done a brake job on her own? Man. Spending your growing-up years in a garage with your dad really didn't prepare you much for the whole man-woman game.

"Is it a deal?" he asked.

She was saved from having to answer him by the sound of a car pulling into her driveway. Marie looked past Davis's shoulder and almost sighed with relief. The cavalry was here. Her little sister, Gina, could always be counted on to monopolize a conversation when a man was around.

Gina jumped out of her compact, slammed the door and ran across the gravel drive to the garage. Dressed in white jeans, a deep green T-shirt and girly sandals that were no more than tiny straps attached to paper-thin soles and completely inappropriate for the weather, she looked like an ad for summer in the middle of the Christmas season. Her short, dark brown hair curled around her head in careless waves that Marie knew took her sister at least an hour to create. Gina's brown eyes lit with undisguised interest as she spotted the sergeant.

"Hi, Marie," she said, never glancing at her sister. "I came to tell you we're going to miss all the good sales if you don't close up now."

Saved! She'd forgotten all about promising to take their nephew Christmas shopping. Grateful for an excuse to get Davis Garvey moving along, she said, "Right. I'll be ready in a second."

"Aren't you going to introduce me?" Gina practically purred, apparently forgetting about the big rush to leave. She didn't bother waiting for an introduction as she walked up to Davis, held her hand out like a Southern belle at a debutante ball and said, "Gina Santini. And you are…?"

"Davis Garvey." He took her hand briefly and gave her a distracted smile.

"You're a marine, aren't you?" Gina asked, smiling.

"That's right." He didn't even look surprised that she'd known his identity as easily as Marie had.

A part of Marie watched in envy as Gina turned on her charm. Honestly, she didn't know how her younger-by-two-years sister did it. Flirting came as easily as breathing to Gina. Her eyes narrowed thoughtfully as she noted the practiced moves. A light touch on Davis's arm. Flipping her hair back with a subtle movement. A ripple of laughter that floated out around them musically.

Marie had been witness to Gina's flirting hundreds of times over the years, and she'd always enjoyed watching the hapless target of her intentions stumble over his tongue. But for some reason, she didn't particularly want to see Davis Garvey reduced to a puddle of drooling male. In fact, for the first time ever, Marie felt a surprising spurt of resentment at her little sister's quick moves.

Honestly, you'd think the girl could have a little self-control. Did she really have to make a conquest wherever she went?

At least though, Marie told herself, the sergeant wouldn't be pretending interest in *her*. Who would, when faced with Gina's more obvious charms?

But, he managed to surprise her again. Far from succumbing to Gina, Davis was actually looking *past* the tiny bundle of dynamite to stare at Marie instead.

A small curl of pure, feminine pleasure floated through her. And when she met Davis's steady gaze, that pleasant feeling thickened and warmed inside her. Good heavens, the man had amazing eyes. And the rest of him wasn't bad, either.

When Gina paused for breath, he said, "If you'll give me the keys to the loaner, I'll leave you my car and you can take off for your shopping."

"Okay." She should have been ashamed of herself. There was a small part of her that was really enjoying Gina's stunned surprise at being overlooked. Smiling, Marie opened a drawer and grabbed up a set of keys.

As he took the keys from her, his fingertips scraped the palm of her hand, sending new bolts of electricity along her nerve endings. Marie curled her fingers into a tight fist and fought to ignore the sensation.

It wasn't easy.

Smiling as if he knew just what she was feeling, he dropped his own keys onto the workbench. "You'll take good care of my car?"

Did his voice really have to take on such an intimate note? Or was she reading more into it than he'd intended? Opting for the latter, and struggling to get her imagination under control, she quipped, "I'll sing it to sleep every night and tuck it in personally."

His eyebrows lifted and one corner of his mouth twitched. "Lucky car."

Her stomach flipped again. Oh, for heaven's sake.

"Two days?" he asked.

"Uh…yes. Two days."

"I'll see you then." Turning, he walked past Gina with a nod. Then he stopped, looked at Marie and said, "Think about lunch."

As he walked slowly to the Volkswagen, Gina stepped up beside her sister. Both women watched him as he fired up the little car and pulled out of the drive onto the street that would take him back to the base.

"Lunch?" Gina asked.

"Yeah."

"He asked you to lunch?"

Why did she say that in the same tone someone would ask, "You were abducted by aliens?"

"Yes, he asked me to lunch." She turned to glare at Gina. "Is that really so hard to believe?"

"'Course not," Gina said, giving her a pat on the shoulder. "You're going, aren't you?"

"No."

"Why not? He's gorgeous."

"He's a customer."

"That is so medieval." Gina crossed to the far corner of the counter, opened a drawer and pulled out one of the candy bars Marie kept stocked there. As she unwrapped the chocolate, she muttered, "You really need to get a life."

"I have a life, thanks." Marie told her and locked the connecting door to the service bay. Then she led her sister outside and walked to Davis's car. She had to pull it into the garage and lock it up. Wouldn't do to take chances with the sergeant's car. After she'd parked the Mustang alongside an ancient Fiat in for a brake job, she got out of the car to discover Gina still talking.

"Okay, then, at the very least, you need glasses. Did you see the way he looked at you?"

"He had to look at me to talk," Marie said briskly. "It's polite."

"Polite had nothing to do with it."

"Cut it out, Gina."

"Me?" She took a bite of candy and waved one hand in the air. "Heck, I gave him my best smile and even fluttered my big baby browns at him and it was like I wasn't there.''

Marie smiled and shook her head. "Just because you're slipping doesn't mean he was interested in me."

"Honey," Gina said, "any man who looks at you like that, despite the fact that you're a *mechanic* of all things, is *not* just being polite."

Pleasure whirled through Marie briefly at the thought. But a moment later, she firmly stomped it into oblivion. She wasn't going to play that game again. Convince herself that a man was interested in her. Indulge in daydreams and wicked fantasies and then have to pick her heart up off the garage floor when reality kicked in.

No, thanks. Been there, done that. Way too many times. Not lately, of course. But her memories of splintered crushes and hurt feelings were vivid.

"Honestly, Marie, don't you *like* men?"

"What's not to like?" she asked, again retreating into humor that was comfortable. Safe.

"Then for pity's sake, make an effort."

"What do you want me to do, little sister? Hit some guy over the head with a socket wrench and drag him into the garage?"

"A woman's gotta do what a woman's gotta do."

"Gina," she said as she keyed in the code in the electric alarm system, pushed her sister out the garage doors, closed them and firmly set the padlock in place, "give it a rest, okay? I'm perfectly happy. Believe it or not, you do not *need* a man to make your life complete."

"Doesn't hurt," Gina mumbled as she finished the candy and stuffed the wrapper into her jeans pocket.

Sure it did, Marie thought. It hurt plenty. Every time she took a chance, only to be flattened by the fist of love, it hurt.

"There's nothing—" she paused for effect "—repeat *nothing* going on here. The sergeant just wants his engine worked on."

Gina's eyebrows wiggled and she grinned at her sister. "I bet it's a real nice engine, too."

A heartbeat passed before Marie laughed. "Good God, girl," she said with a shake of her head, "take a pill. Your hormones are in overdrive again."

"Better overdrive than stalled."

This is what she had to put up with because she'd loaned her car to Mama. Putting up with Gina should be enough to curb future bouts of generosity.

"My hormones are just fine. Thanks for your concern."

"Sometimes, Marie," Gina said thoughtfully as they walked to her car, "I wonder if you even *have* hormones."

Oh, she thought as they pulled out of the driveway and headed toward home, she had them all right. At the moment, in fact, they were all standing straight up and screaming at her.

But she'd had a lot of practice at taming them, and she had no doubt she could do it again. Although, she admitted silently as the scenery whizzed past, Davis Garvey was more of a challenge than she'd ever had to face before.

"Cheer up, sis," Gina said on a laugh, "maybe Santa will leave you a marine in your stocking!"

Oh, now, *there* was a mental image.

Davis drove through the guard gate, nodded at the sentries and ignored their barely muffled snorts of laughter. Okay, so the Volkswagen looked like hell. Its engine purred like a kitten.

Amazing woman.

Not only did she kick-start his body into high gear, she knew cars, too. He could really get to like Marie Santini.

But even as he thought it, alarm bells went off in his head. Having a nice, mutually satisfying affair was one thing. Actually getting emotionally involved was something else again. He didn't want to *like* her. It was enough that he simply *wanted* her. Just touching her hand had given him as big a rush as surviving that test drive.

Marie Santini definitely had his attention. And what was wrong with a hot, satisfying, temporary relationship?

Camp Pendleton would be his home for the next three years or so. After that, he'd be reassigned. He made a point of never getting so involved, he couldn't walk away easily. Because Davis *always* walked away.

One of the things he liked best about being in the corps was the fact that rootless types like him fit right in. There was no room for roots in the marines. You went in, did your job, then moved on. All in all, a good way to live your life. See the world and never have to stay in one spot long enough to notice you don't fit in.

He dismissed that train of thought, turned the steering wheel and drove along the nearly empty road, headed for the NCO barracks. He passed a fast-food place, a small, tidy-looking church and a basketball court where a dozen or so kids raced back and forth across the asphalt. In the winter twilight, multi-colored Christmas lights twinkled on rooftops, around windows and in the bare branches of trees.

Christmas again. The one time of year he almost envied his married buddies. But the season would pass soon, as would those brief longings for something more in his life.

Pulling into a parking slot, he got out, locked the car and headed for his apartment. One that looked much like every other place he'd lived in for the last fifteen years.

Before he could open the front door though, his neighbor, Sergeant Mike Coffey, stepped out of his place and said with a pointed look at the VW, "I see you found Santini's."

"Recognize the loaner, do you?"

"Hell, yes." Mike grinned. "Drove it myself last month."

Pocketing his keys, Davis cocked his head and looked at the other man. "So how come you didn't tell me your Miracle Worker was a good-looking woman?"

"Good-looking?" Mike asked with a shrug. "To tell you the truth, I never really noticed."

How could he not have noticed those green eyes

and the suggestion of a dimple in her cheek? Was Coffey blind or was Davis nuts?

"Doesn't really matter what she looks like," Mike was saying, "she's a whiz with cars."

Hmm. Maybe it didn't matter to Mike, but Davis could still see her in his mind's eye. Still, he didn't admit to it. "She'd better be," he said.

Mike laughed. "Don't worry. Your Mustang's perfectly safe."

Don't worry? Hell, Davis was extremely picky about who worked on the Mustang. Or any of the other cars he had tucked away in storage garages all across the country. Then he remembered Marie's confident smile and the concentration on her face when she listened to the rumbling of his car's engine. He had a feeling Mike was right. He didn't have anything to worry about. As far as his car was concerned, anyway.

"Trust me," Mike said. "Once Marie works on your car, you'll never want anyone else's hands touching it."

The other man gave him a wave and ducked back into his own apartment. Davis stood there in the lowering darkness for a long minute and thought about Marie Santini's hands. Strong, slender, delicate, capable.

And he had to admit, it wasn't just his cars he was thinking about her hands being on.

Three

Could she really kill her sister at the dinner table? Sure she could, Marie told herself silently. But someone was sure to notice.

"I'm talkin' *hunk* here," Gina said emphatically, and plopped down into her chair at the dinner table. "I swear, if he wasn't a marine, he could be a model or something."

Marie gritted her teeth, set the salad bowl down on the dining room table and walked to her seat. She shouldn't have agreed to eat with the family tonight. Should have known that Gina would still be talking about Davis Garvey. Heck, she'd been talking about him all afternoon. Even shopping in the crowded mall hadn't shut her up.

With a mental sigh, she thought longingly of the peace and quiet of her garage apartment.

"We understand, dear," Maryann Santini said, and smiled at her youngest daughter. "He's handsome."

"Beyond handsome," Gina corrected, and slanted a look at Marie. "Wouldn't you say so?"

If given the chance, which she hadn't been, Marie might have said a lot of things. Like, he wasn't really handsome in the traditional sense, but he had a sort of inner strength that appealed to her—and apparently Gina. But all she said was, "I think you've already said plenty on the subject."

Far from looking abashed, Gina just grinned. "All I'm saying is that he's one hot property and he was looking at Marie like she was the last steak at a barbecue."

"Thank you so much for the lovely analogy." But she couldn't help thinking that Gina had seen one too many movies. Although a part of her wanted to believe that the first sergeant had been interested, another, more rational part reminded her that she wasn't the girl guys asked out. She was the girl guys talked to about *other* girls.

"So is he a nice young man?" Mama asked, eyebrows lifted into high arches, her gaze locked on her middle daughter.

Marie stifled a sigh. If he looked like a gargoyle, Mama wouldn't care as long as he was "nice." Being Italian wouldn't hurt, either.

Better to head her mother off at the pass. Maryann Santini loved a good romance better than anything. And the only thing worse than having to live with her own disappointing love life was knowing that her mother had given up all hope of Marie finding a boyfriend.

According to Mama, feminism was all well and good—but it would never take the place of a big wedding and lots of kids.

"For heaven's sake," Marie sputtered. "How do I know if he's nice? I just met the man. And he's not up for grabs, either," she said with a pointed look at her little sister. "I'm just fixing his car. That's all. End of story."

Gina snorted.

"He seems taken with you," Mama argued.

"According to Gina." She slid her gaze toward the tiny brunette across the table from her. Justifiable homicide. No jury of big sisters would ever convict her.

"Gina's very wise about these things," Mama said, giving her youngest daughter a quick smile of approval.

Meaning, of course, that Gina knew how to catch a man's eye. Something Mama had given up on teaching Marie years ago. Apparently though, old hopes die hard.

"No one's asked me," Angela, the oldest of the Santini girls said quietly, "but who cares if he's interested? It's obvious that Marie is *not*."

"Thank you," Marie said heartily, surprised, but pleased at the support. "At last a voice of reason."

"Besides," Angela went on as she poured her son, Jeremy, a glass of milk, "Gina was probably wrong. After all, when she's at work, Marie's hardly the stuff men's fantasies are made of. All that grease and grime... What man is going to take the trouble to look past the surface?''

Well, thanks again, she thought, but didn't say.

''I can solve that,'' Marie said lightly. ''I'll just wear one of your old prom queen dresses the next time I rebuild a carburetor. Oh, and maybe a small, but tasteful tiara. Just think how the diamonds will twinkle in the fluorescent lights.''

''Funny,'' Angela muttered.

''I like Aunt Marie just how she is,'' Jeremy piped up.

She sent him a grin and a wink. ''Have I told you lately that you are my absolute favorite eight-year-old person?''

''Yep,'' he said. ''But I think you should tell Santa, just to be sure *he* knows, too.''

''Count on it, buddy,'' she said. If it struck her as just a little sad that her most ardent male admirer was her nephew, Marie buried the jab quickly.

Her mother and sisters continued to talk around her, but she stopped paying attention. It didn't matter what they thought, she told herself as she concentrated on getting through dinner as quickly as possible. But, of course, it did matter. Always had.

And that was both the blessing and the curse of being a member of a close family.

She glanced at the familiar faces seated around the dining table that had been in the Santini family since God was a boy. The solid mahogany table shone from years of polish and bore the scratches of innumerable generations of Santinis like badges of honor.

There was Gina, always perky enough for three cheerleaders. Angela, pretty but quieter, sadder since being widowed three years before. Jeremy, bustling through life with all the grace of the proverbial bull in a china shop. And Mama—patient, loving, *there*.

She missed her dad. A pang of old sorrow twisted around her heart briefly. Two years he'd been gone now. Papa had been the one male in Marie's life to really appreciate her.

A tomboy from the time she could walk, Marie had grown up in Santini's garage. She'd been the son Papa'd never had. And though she'd loved her special relationship with her father, she'd always been sorry that she and her mom weren't closer. Angela, Gina and Mama had shared girly things, and though Marie had sometimes wistfully watched them all from the sidelines, she had never really felt comfortable enough to try and join in.

Still, she thought, letting go of old regrets, they were family. And family—love—was all-important and always there.

As much as they drove her nuts, Gina knew she'd be lost without them. A sudden, unexpected sting of tears tickled the backs of her eyes. Family. Tradition. Roots. The Santinis were big on all of them, and that was a good thing, wasn't it? To know that there were people who loved you, supported you, no matter what?

She nodded to herself, feeling much more magnanimous toward them all.

"So!" Gina spoke up loudly to get her attention. "If Marie's not interested, like she claims, I say she brings the hunk home to dinner so we can have a shot at him.''

So much for magnanimity.

"The man's not a prize turkey, you know," Marie snapped.

"Me thinks she doth protest too much," Gina said.

"Oh, for heaven's sake," Marie told her in irritation, "he's not the last living man on the planet. Why are you so intent on him?"

"Why are you so defensive?"

"I'm not." Was she? An uncomfortable thought. After all, what did it matter to her if Gina made a move on him?

She shifted uneasily in her chair.

"Good," Gina said with a brisk nod. "Then it's settled. You'll bring him to dinner. What's good for you, Mom?" she asked. "Saturday?"

"Saturday's fine, if Marie's sure."

"Marie didn't agree to any of this," Marie pointed out.

"You will, though," Angela said, "if only to prove to Gina that you don't care."

She shot her sister a nasty look, mainly because she was right. "Fine. Saturday. I'll invite him." And feel like a fool for asking a perfect stranger home for a family dinner. "Happy, now?"

Gina smiled. Angela nodded. Mama was already planning the menu.

Marie sat back in her chair and glared at all of them.

You know, maybe family was overrated.

* * *

Davis held down the channel button on the remote and idly stared at the TV as images flipped on and off the screen. He really wasn't in the mood to watch; it was simply something to do. In the darkness, the rapidly changing pictures and sounds dispelled the quiet emptiness of his apartment.

Not that he was lonely, he assured himself. Far from it. He set the remote down on the table and picked up the carton of cold chow mein that was his dinner. Propping his feet up on the coffee table, he stared blankly at the screen, not really interested in the life cycle of the honeybee.

He liked his life. He liked being able to eat in the living room right out of the carton. If the place was a mess, there was no one around to complain. He liked not having to unpack his moving boxes until he was good and ready—which usually meant two or three months. Liked moving to new bases every few years. Seeing new faces, new places.

New faces. Instantly one particular face rose up in his mind—as it had all evening. Marie Santini.

He'd never spent so much time thinking about a woman he hardly knew. Whether it was her big green eyes or the adrenaline rush her driving gave him, something about her had hit him hard. Hard enough to make him rethink that casual invitation to lunch. If spending less than a half hour with her was enough to get him thinking about her, did he really want to pursue this?

He much preferred a simple, no-ties-involved relationship. And Marie Santini was practically encircled by a white picket fence. Everything about her screamed out hearth and home. Altogether a dangerous female.

But then, marines were supposed to thrive on danger, right?

A knock on the door exploded his thoughts and he was grateful for the distraction. Setting the carton of chow mein down with relief, he walked across the room and opened the door.

"Hey," Mike Coffey said, "a couple of us are going into town for dinner. Want to come?"

Davis glanced over his shoulder at the darkened room, the flickering TV and the half-eaten chow mein container. There was such a thing as too much time to yourself, he thought, and suddenly he wanted out of that too-quiet, too-lonely apartment. "Yeah. Just let me turn off the TV."

She had plenty of work to do.

And she would do it, she promised herself, just as soon as Davis Garvey had picked up his car and was gone again. Until then, she kept busy at her desk.

Marie hated paperwork. She'd much rather be under a car than hunched over a computer. Unfortunately she didn't have a car to work on at the moment. Jim Bester had picked up his Fiat that morning and Davis Garvey would soon be by to pick up the Mustang. Apparently, every other automobile in Bayside had decided to stay healthy throughout the Christmas season.

Davis.

As soon as he got there, she'd have to ask him to dinner.

Grumbling to herself, she tossed her pen down onto the desk and stood up. She never should have given in to Gina's goading. Why in heaven would Davis even *want* to come to dinner at her house? For Pete's sake, the man wasn't going to want to sit down with a bunch of strangers.

Although, she thought as she marched into the service bay and flicked on the overhead lights, the idea wasn't as strange as some might think. Every year around the holidays, an informal Adopt A Marine program started up. Families in town would invite young marines away from home to holiday dinners, so they wouldn't be stuck on base eating in the commissary. Her own family had participated a few times over the years and it had always worked out well. The marines were grateful for a respite from the base and the families enjoyed the company of some lonely young men. She supposed she could think of Davis in that context.

Sure. Why not? Just imagine him a lonely marine away from his own family at a special time of year. The fact that he didn't look like the image of a lonely young soldier didn't really have to come into this. Did it?

"Besides, it's Christmas," she said aloud, her voice echoing slightly in the empty service bay.

"According to my watch," a familiar, deep voice said from the open doorway behind her, "we still have about three weeks until Christmas."

Surprised, Marie jumped and turned around to

face him. "Do the marines teach you to sneak up on unsuspecting civilians?"

"Oh, yeah," he said, walking toward her until he was stopped just inches from her. "Sneaking 101. A very popular course."

Too close, she thought. He was standing way too close for comfort. She could smell the sharp, citrusy scent of his aftershave and see a small nick beneath his chin where he'd cut himself shaving.

And what was going on with her stomach, pitching and rolling like she was on a roller coaster? "Well," she said, trying to get a grip. "I hope your teacher gave you an A."

"An A plus, actually." He moved closer still and Marie took a short half step backward. "They like us to be able to walk quiet in our line of work."

"Yeah," she said. "It probably comes in handy. In a jungle."

He laughed and Marie didn't even want to admit to herself what a nice sound it was.

"So," he asked, "my car ready?"

"Yes," she said. "It is." And the sooner he took it, the better. She'd spent way too much time already thinking about him. The last two days, his face had cropped up in her mind far too often for comfort.

"Good." He reached out and laid one hand on her forearm. Even through her sweater's bulky material, a series of small electrical charges pulsed through her. Marie's breath caught and she pulled away, stepping around him to lead him into the office. Mentally she did the multiplication tables in a futile effort to reclaim her mind.

As she walked behind the counter, he took up position directly opposite her. Laying his palms flat atop the laminate surface, he waited for her to look at him, then asked, "So how about lunch?"

"No thanks," she said and stopped silently counting at four times twelve. If she went out to lunch with him, that would mean she was interested in him. Which she wasn't. Besides, with her stomach twisting and untwisting, who could eat?

"I remember," he said. "You don't date your customers."

"No, that's not it," she said quickly before she could lose her nerve. Just ask him, she told herself. Ask him to come to dinner and prove to her sisters *and* to Mama that she wasn't attracted to him. Heck. Maybe she could prove it to herself, too. "I just thought maybe you'd like to have dinner tonight instead. At my house."

Davis just looked at her for a long moment. He'd told himself all the way over here that he wasn't going to repeat the invitation to lunch. Any woman who interested him this much this quickly was one to stay clear of.

But then he'd seen her again. Stood close enough to catch a whiff of the flowery scent she wore. Looked down into those green eyes and had known that he had to spend more time with her. Risky or not.

Still, he couldn't help wondering what had changed her mind. A couple of days ago, she wouldn't go out to lunch with him. Now she's inviting him to a cozy dinner at her place?

Marie Santini was one confusing woman, he thought. But as his gaze swept over her again, he told himself it would be interesting trying to figure her out.

"Well?" she prompted.

"Sure," he said. "I'd like that."

She inhaled deeply and blew the air out in a rush again. "Good."

"What time?" he asked, smiling at her obvious signs of nervousness.

"Oh. Six, I guess." She picked up a pad of paper and scribbled down the address.

When he took it from her, his fingertips brushed across hers and instantly, tendrils of heat exploded between them.

She yanked her hand back as if she'd been burned by that same blast of energy, and Davis wondered if he was doing the right thing. If they set sparks off each other that easily, could a fire be far behind?

Four

So much for a cozy dinner for two.

He should have known better. Should have guessed that she was up to something. Marie had gone from refusing his lunch invitation to inviting him to dinner at her home. And he'd already noticed that she didn't seem the type to move fast and loose.

But who would have figured on this? His gaze flicked across the faces gathered around the oblong dining table. Gina, the flirty brunette he'd met earlier at the garage. Angela, the eldest, a stunning widow and the mother of Jeremy, an eight-year-old who would one day make a great interrogator. The kid never ran out of questions. At the end of the table sat Maryann Santini—Mama. Her green eyes were the image of Marie's and had hardly left him in the last hour.

He shot a glance at Marie on his right and wondered why she hadn't told him she'd be throwing him into a family dinner.

Of course, if she had, he wouldn't have come. He'd never been comfortable around families. He'd always felt like a kid standing outside a candy store. He could see good stuff inside—he just couldn't get to it. After a while he'd stopped looking.

"So," Jeremy piped up from the other end of the table, "how come you're not wearing a uniform, and where's your gun?"

Clearly Davis's khaki slacks and pale blue sportshirt were a big disappointment to the kid. "I don't usually wear the uniform off base and we don't bring guns to dinner."

"Man, what a rip-off," the boy muttered.

He knew exactly how the kid felt. He'd expected candlelight, a bottle of wine and some quiet conversation. Just him and Marie. What a rip-off.

"That's enough," the boy's mother said, and turned a smile on Davis. "So how long have you been at Camp Pendleton, Davis?"

"Just about a week, ma'am," he said, concentrating on finishing dinner. He had to get out of there.

"And where are you from?"

He took another bite of lasagna, and when he'd swallowed, answered, "My last posting was in North Carolina."

"No," Gina said, giving him one of those practiced, flirty looks she'd been sending him all evening. Damn, the girl was good. Too bad he wasn't interested. For some reason, Gina's obvious sexuality didn't have near the appeal for Davis as Marie's inherent sensuality.

She continued talking, though, and Davis couldn't think of a way to stop her. "My sister meant, where are you from originally?"

His fingers tightened around his fork. Everywhere, he thought. Nowhere.

"Where's your family?" Marie's mom asked.

"I don't have a family, ma'am," he said, and hoped they'd leave it at that.

He should have known better. For the last hour, the Santini women had been pumping him for information about the base, the corps in general and himself specifically. All of them but Marie, that is. The woman he'd come to see had hardly spoken to him. He shot another look at her. Her green eyes met his briefly and once again he felt that indefinable something that coursed between them.

He shouldn't have given in to the impulse to come here tonight. Hell, he'd known from the get-go that he shouldn't be seeing her. Just pulling up in front of her house had told him that.

It was an old Craftsman-style with a wide front porch and a big bay window, through which lamplight poured out into the darkness. A rainbow of Christmas lights were strung across every surface. Every bush sparkled, and the porch pillar posts were wrapped with strings of flickering lights that seemed to move like those on an old movie marquee. On the roof, Santa's sleigh had slipped to a precarious angle and a couple of his reindeer looked ready to fall. Hell, it had been like looking at a Christmas card. An advertisement for cozy warmth and home fires burning. He wasn't used to dealing with women so grounded. So rooted. He preferred impersonal apartments and women who recognized the beauty of a brief, but mutually satisfying affair.

So what was he doing here? Mistake, he thought. Big mistake.

Marie Santini and he came from two different worlds and it would be easier for both of them if they stayed that way.

"No family?" Mama Santini repeated with a shake of her head. "I'm so sorry. You must miss them terribly. Especially at this time of year."

He didn't say anything and wondered what she would think if he told her you couldn't miss something you'd never had. But she wouldn't understand that. None of them would. How could they?

"You won't spend Christmas alone, will you?" Gina asked.

"Oh, no," Mama put in before he could answer. "You'll come here."

He choked on a bite of lasagna and had to force it down with a gulp of wine. Spend Christmas with the Santini women? He didn't think so. Three eager faces watched him as he tried desperately to come up with an excuse that would get him out of this without offending them.

Marie had been quiet all evening, as if to prove to her too-inquisitive family that she wasn't the slightest bit interested in Davis Garvey. She'd sat by while Mama and Angela grilled him. While Gina batted her eyelashes and coyly smiled. While even Jeremy quizzed the poor man about everything marine.

But the look on Davis's face told her that the family had gone too far. She didn't know what it was about the mention of family that had shuttered his feature, but she figured it wasn't any of hers— or her family's business.

"You know what?" Marie spoke up, changing the subject, and the other three women looked at her. "It's getting late. I've gotta get Jeremy to the batting cages."

"Cool!" her nephew shouted, and jumped out of his chair.

"Yes," his mother called out after him, "you can be excused."

"Batting cages?" Davis asked, clearly grateful for the shift in conversation. "In December?"

"Sign-ups for Little League are in February," she told him and stood up. "Gotta get in shape."

As she'd expected, Davis took the opportunity she'd handed him.

He pushed himself up from the table and stood beside her. "I think I'll be going, too, but thank you for dinner, Mrs. Santini."

"Call me Mama," she said. "Everyone does."

He actually paled.

Apparently the combined forces of the Santini women could bring even a marine to his knees.

They escaped the dining room together and headed for the front door. Behind them, three female voices broke into a whispered conversation. From upstairs came the sound of Jeremy's running feet and Marie knew she only had a minute or two to get rid of Davis.

And she did want to get rid of him, she reminded herself.

She walked him to the door and opened it. "Thanks for coming," she said.

But he didn't leave. He only stood there, looking down at her. "Why didn't you tell me?" he asked.

"Tell you?"

He shook his head. "About your whole family being here?"

"Oh," she said with what she hoped was a convincingly innocent tone, "didn't I?"

"No."

"Okay," Marie said, and tightly gripped the doorknob with her right hand. Watching him at the table had stirred up a bit of guilt inside her. He'd looked so ill at ease, she'd almost felt sorry for him when the questioning had gotten fast and furious. "I should have told you. But Gina wanted to see you again and I thought…"

His eyes widened and he chuckled under his breath. The sound had a strange effect on her. Almost as if it had danced along her spine, sending goose bumps trailing across her flesh. She took a slow, deep breath and told herself—*again*—to get a grip.

"So you were trying to set me up with your sister?"

"What's wrong with my sister?" she demanded, instinctively defensive, despite the fact that only a few minutes ago, she'd wanted to kill Gina for pouncing on the man.

"Nothing that a couple dozen Valium wouldn't cure," he muttered. Then he asked, "Is she *always* so perky?"

Marie ducked her head to hide a smile. Gina's perpetual cheerleader attitude could get a little wearing. "She has a positive personality."

"You could say that," he said, and moved in a little closer. "But," he reminded her quietly, "I didn't ask her to lunch. I asked you."

"And I asked you to dinner. So we're even."

"Not yet," he said.

Did he practice giving women that long, soulful look? Or was it a gift he was born with? Marie's breath hitched in her chest. He seemed to loom over her—and she wasn't exactly on the petite side. But Sergeant Garvey was not only tall, he was broad, and from what she could see, in fantastic shape.

She was way out of her depth.

"Look," she said, drawing in a deep breath, but keeping her voice low enough so that her family wouldn't overhear her, "why are you doing this?"

"Doing what?" He actually sounded confused.

"This. Acting like you're interested in me."

"Who's acting?" he asked, and lifted one hand to smooth her hair back from her face. The slightest touch of his fingertips sent short bursts of excitement fluttering through her, and Marie took one hasty step back.

All night she'd watched him, listened to him and tried to remember that she wasn't attracted to him.

Wasn't interested in him. So why did he have to touch her and shoot all of her fine notions clear to the moon?

"You ready, Marie?" Jeremy called, and thundered down the stairs and past them out the door.

"Yes," she yelled after him gratefully. And then to her family she called, "We'll be back in an hour or so."

Davis followed her onto the porch, and in the glow of the Christmas lights, he asked, "So where are the batting cages?"

"Why?" she responded warily.

He shrugged. "It's been a long time since I've done any hitting. Thought it might be fun."

Oh, for heaven's sake.

With her hair pulled back into a ponytail, she looked about seventeen. And entirely too good.

Davis stood outside the cage, curling his fingers into the wire mesh as he watched Marie teach her nephew the proper batting stance. His gaze followed every wiggle of her hips, and the curve of her behind in those tight black jeans was enough to stop his heart.

She'd paid no attention to him at all since they'd arrived at the cages. Every bit of her concentration was on the nephew who clearly adored her. She was patient, firm and surprisingly knowledgeable about the intricacies of batting.

Along the line of cages, baseballs thumped into the netting and slammed against wooden backboards. Piped in from overhead speakers came a stream of Christmas carols, and the cold ocean air whipping over the crowds gave the whole place a seasonal feel.

Dozens of kids ran loose, their harried-looking parents handing out quarters for the cages and the video machines. It had been years since Davis had been to one of these places and he found himself enjoying it. He took a last gulp of really bad coffee, crushed the now-empty hot cup, tossed it into the trash and turned his attention back to Marie.

He couldn't help himself. She captivated him, and that was a bad sign, he knew. He should have gone home and forgotten all about the sexy mechanic. But even knowing that, he hadn't been able to leave her yet. Damn. It was like going into combat. You knew it was dangerous and your gut told you to run like hell. But a stronger instinct—something primal and undeniable—took over, making you stand your ground.

And a purely male instinct was telling him to grab Marie and kiss her so long and hard and deep that neither of them would worry about the consequences.

She fitted the batting helmet on Jeremy's head, patted the top and then slipped out of the cage, closing the door behind her.

"Okay, kiddo," she called out. "Get ready. The first one's coming in hard and fast."

"I know, I know," the boy answered in that patient tone that all kids adopt when talking to adults.

"You're good with him," Davis said, sliding a look at her.

"He's a great kid." She shrugged, keeping her eyes on Jeremy. The first pitch went past him. "Keep your swing even."

"So how'd you learn so much about baseball?" Davis asked, more for something to talk about than anything else.

"My dad taught me," she said. Then she called out, "you have to keep both hands on the bat."

"I didn't think little girls played baseball."

She shot him a glance, and smiled and said, "Welcome to the twentieth century."

"Baseball and auto repair, huh?"

"What can I say? I'm a Renaissance woman."

She was that.

"Did your sisters play, too?" He didn't care about her sisters. He just wanted to hear that smoky-sounding voice of hers again.

Marie laughed and shook her head, still watching Jeremy. She clucked her tongue when the kid missed another pitch. "Angela and Gina? Play baseball? No way."

"So you were the tomboy in the bunch?"

"Were?" She shook her head. "Still am." She winced when Jeremy took a pitch on his arm. "Rub it out, kiddo, and get ready for the next one."

She intrigued him completely. He'd never known anyone quite like her. The women he dated wouldn't be caught dead playing ball with a bunch of kids. Marie seemed to thrive on it. She was just so damned *alive*.

"You're patient, too," Davis commented.

She turned a quizzical look on him. "You expected me to slap Jeremy around?"

"No," he said with a smile. "But usually adults get a little testy—start yelling—when a kid's not learning."

"Speaking from experience, are we?" she asked.

When he didn't answer, Marie looked up at him, and he felt as though she was looking deep inside him. To where he kept his secrets. And he didn't like it.

He shifted, tearing his gaze from hers and effectively cutting off any question she might have asked. He didn't want to talk—or think—about his past. He wanted to talk about the now. With her.

"Hey, Santini!" A deep voice called out from just behind them.

Davis glanced over his shoulder in time to see a tall, hulking guy step up next to Marie and give her behind a swat. She yelped and Davis took a step closer, to put himself between her and the guy who'd actually hit her. Instinct had his right hand curling into a fist even as Marie turned, rubbing her bottom with one hand and grinned at the guy.

"Nicky, hi! I didn't know you were back in town."

His fisted hand relaxed but that didn't mean his guts weren't still churning. Just who the hell was this guy, and how did he have the right to be slapping Marie's butt?

"Davis, this is Nick Cassaccio. An old friend."

"Hi," Nick said, and offered a hand to Davis. He

took it, but kept a wary eye on the guy anyway. Just how old and how good a friend was he?

"So how'd it go with Patty?" she asked.

"Just like you said," Nick told her on a big smile.

"Good, I'm glad."

"Yeah, me, too." He reached out tugged her ponytail and said, "I gotta be going, brat. Just wanted to say hi."

"See you, Nick," she called after him as he drifted off into the crowd.

"Brat?"

Marie shrugged. "He's always called me that."

Davis frowned. How long was *always?* "Who's Patty?"

"Nick's girlfriend. Well," she corrected herself, "fiancée, now, I guess."

"Oh." That's good. But if the guy was after some other woman, what's he doing slapping Marie's behind? And most important, he demanded silently, why the hell did *he* care?

He didn't. No. It had been purely instinct to want to hit a man who'd hit a woman. It had nothing to do with the woman in question being Marie. Right. Even he didn't believe that.

"So what was he thanking you for?"

Marie gave him a quick look, then turned her attention back to Jeremy. "Nothing, really. Patty broke up with him and he came over to the garage whining about it, and I told him that she was probably tired of waiting for him to pop the question."

"So he popped?"

She grinned. "Apparently."

Davis's eyebrows arched. "Batting instructor, mechanic and giver of advice to the lovelorn?"

"I am a woman of many talents," she said lightly.

"I do believe I agree with you," Davis told her and watched as her small smile faded into a look that was part nerves, part excitement. He reached out and ran one finger across the nape of her neck. She shivered and that tremor rocked him, too. "So," he asked, his voice low and suddenly thick, "what advice would Dear Marie have for me?"

She shrugged his hand off and looked up at him from beneath lowered lashes. "I guess I'd have to tell you to stop working so hard to convince me you're interested. And to move on to greener pastures."

"Maybe I don't see any pastures greener."

"Then you should have your eyes checked."

Does she really not know how attractive she is? he wondered. "My eyes work just fine," he said. Then he asked, "And what makes you think I'm not interested?"

She gave a short, strained laugh. "I've never exactly been the belle of the ball, sergeant. Men don't usually chase me down the street shouting their undying love."

Why the hell not? he wondered, but didn't ask. Instead he said, "Maybe you just haven't been listening."

"Yeah?" she said pointedly. "Same to you."

He grinned. Whether he should or shouldn't, Davis knew that he wouldn't be staying away from her.

Trouble or not, he had to see this through, wherever it led.

"Aunt Marie," Jeremy called from the cage, "I'm not getting it."

"Just keep your swing even, sweetie."

Davis looked at the kid and mentally flashed back to his own childhood. When he'd wanted to be in Little League more than anything. When the thought of belonging to a team and being good at something was the most important thing in the world.

But his childhood had been different from Jeremy's. Growing up in a series of foster homes where he was never sure from one week to the next where he'd be living, Davis hadn't been much of a joiner.

Until the corps. Now he *did* belong somewhere and the past couldn't touch him anymore.

He shook off old thoughts and stepped past Marie into the cage. "Try this," he said, and positioned the boy's hands on the bat. Then drawing Jeremy's arms back, he showed him exactly how to hit high and away.

When he rejoined Marie outside the cage, he fed another quarter into the slot. He really didn't want to think about how good it felt to be here. With her and the boy.

He just wanted to enjoy it.

The next pitch came and Jeremy connected solidly, sending the baseball high into the overhead nets. Excited, he turned around, beaming at them. "Did you see it? Did you see how far I hit that?"

"You bet I did," Marie said.

"Do it again, kid," Davis told him.

"Just watch me," Jeremy yelled and turned around to face the pitching machine.

"Thanks," Marie whispered.

"No problem," Davis answered, and enjoyed the first real smile she'd given him.

Five

"Thanks, Davis," Jeremy said, "that was great!"

The kid was bouncing with excess energy. Davis knew marines who didn't have as much get-up-and-go as this small boy. And the kid didn't quit, either. Even when he wasn't doing well at the cages, he hadn't stomped off. He'd just set his feet and tried harder. There were a few privates on base who could learn a lesson from this boy.

A cold ocean wind rattled the naked branches of the tree standing sentry in the front yard and set the strings of Christmas lights swaying. The motion left a rainbow pattern of sliding lights trailing across the front of the house.

"You did good, kid," Davis said with a smile.

"You wanna hit some more balls tomorrow?" the

boy asked, hopping from one foot to the other in his eagerness to recapture the glow of slamming a homer in the batting cages.

Davis paused before answering, mainly because he didn't know what to say. And in that pause, Marie jumped in to fill the silence.

"Sergeant Garvey doesn't have time to take you to the cages, Jeremy." She reached out to ruffle the boy's hair. "You and I will go again soon, okay?"

Jeremy ducked his head, then squinted up at Davis. "If you're not too busy, you could always just come anyways, though, right?"

"We'll see how it goes, okay?" A stall. Perfect. Why didn't he just tell the kid flat-out that he wasn't interested in an unofficial Big Brother program? He was only here to see Marie. He'd never had any intention of getting to know her family.

As if she knew what he was thinking, Marie gave him a cool look before turning to her nephew. "Go on in now, Jeremy. Your mom's probably wondering where you are."

The boy nodded and headed across the lawn toward the house. Before he climbed the front steps though, he turned back and yelled, "Remember, tomorrow...just in case."

Davis lifted one hand in acknowledgment, but it was so dark, he doubted the kid saw him. Once the boy was inside, Davis slid a glance at Marie, standing beside him. It was the first time he'd actually been *alone* with her all night. This *date* hadn't exactly gone as planned, he thought, but standing here with her in the cold winter night, he didn't really mind.

Her scent drifted to him on the breeze and everything inside him felt as though he was going on full alert. Every sense was heightened, every breath seemed measured. She stared at him and he wished he could see every emotion flickering in the depths of her green eyes. But the light wasn't strong enough. There was only the darkness and the soft wind blowing around them.

Then she spoke and the spell was shattered.

"So," she said in a too-hearty voice, "thanks for everything and maybe I'll see you around."

In other words, *Shove off, Sergeant.*

"Around where?" he asked, just to hear her voice again.

"Just…around." She shrugged. "It's a small town."

Not good enough. He suddenly wanted to know when he was going to see her again. "What if I asked you to dinner? Just the two of us this time."

"Why would you do that?"

Why indeed? He should be climbing into his car and heading for the base. But he wasn't ready to leave just yet. He'd come here tonight to see her. And he hadn't had more than a minute or two of her time all night. Davis wasn't used to sharing.

He took a step closer to her, and even in the darkness, he saw wariness flicker in her eyes. That bothered him more than he wanted to admit. Damn it, what was there to be wary of? "Let's just say I'd like to spend time with you. Alone."

She laughed, and it was a second or two before he heard the nervous note in that chuckle. "You don't have to do this," she said. "Your car's fixed. No reason to smooth-talk the mechanic."

Davis frowned slightly. "Who said anything about my car?"

"Look," Marie said, and backed up a step or two. "I appreciate your being so nice to Jeremy...." her words picked up steam until she was nearly babbling. "I mean, your showing him how to hit a fly ball was really great. I've been concentrating on showing him an even swing, so he could lock into solid base hits. But I guess every kid wants to blast a grand slam...."

"I guess," he agreed, and moved with her as she started to cross the lawn. "But I really don't want to talk about Jeremy at the moment."

"Apparently not," she muttered, and sighed heavily. "You're just not going to leave, are you?"

He smiled at her. "Not until I walk you to your door," he said, then glanced at the front of the house off to his left. "Which, by the way, is over there."

"Yeah," she told him and pointed down the driveway toward the frame, two-storied garage. "But I live there. In an apartment upstairs."

"Good," he said, glad to know he and Marie could have a little quiet time without her family hanging in doorways. Now all he had to do was convince her that she wanted a little quiet time with him.

They walked along the side of the house, the only illumination the overhead Christmas lights and a moon that peeked in and out from behind rain clouds.

At the foot of the stairs, she stopped, turned around and held out one hand toward him. "Okay, Sergeant. Mission accomplished. I'm at my door. Good night."

He took her hand and instantly felt a swell of heat dance from her fingertips to his. That heat rushed along his arm and settled in his chest, filling him with a sort of warmth he'd never felt before. She felt it, too; he knew it. Even in the shadows, he saw her reaction written plainly on her face.

His thumb stroked the back of her hand when she tried to pull free. He didn't want to break that connection just yet. Didn't want to lose the warmth still pulsing inside him.

"Technically," he whispered, "you're not at your door yet."

"Who pays attention to technicalities?" she asked, and he heard the slight tremor in her voice.

"Marines," he answered. "And mechanics."

She licked her lips and took a backward step up onto the stairs. He followed her.

"What is it you're after?" she asked quietly, still halfheartedly trying to tug her hand free of his grasp. "Bucking for a discount oil change?"

Did she really think a man would be interested in her solely for her mechanical abilities?

"What do you think?" he asked.

Another step up, toward the door on the landing.

"I think you've got the wrong Santini," she said. "Gina's in the house. I could go get her for you."

He shook his head. "I didn't come here tonight to see Gina." Her younger sister might be a nice woman, but she never shut up long enough for him to be sure. "Hell," he added, "I thought dinner was going to be just you and me. But you knew that, didn't you?"

Another step backward and Marie almost stumbled. Just what she needed—to go pitching headfirst down the flight of stairs. She'd probably kill him in her fall and have the entire Marine Corps down on her for knocking off one of their sergeants. On the other hand, if she didn't kill him, they'd end up at the bottom of the steps, all wrapped up together. Arms and legs touching, bodies pressed tight. Oh, my...

If he'd only let go of her hand, maybe she could think straight. But his grip didn't lessen and the ridiculous spurts of heat she'd felt at that first contact with his skin showed no signs of tapering off. Another step up. Careful, Marie, careful.

Oh, jeez, she thought as she drew in a long, steadying breath. He smelled like Old Spice, marine and—she took another whiff—*trouble*. Now she knew what it felt like to be an opposing army in those old war movies. Marines never retreated. Always advancing. Always closer. And closer. The poor bad guys never stood a chance.

"So tell me," he said, still climbing the stairs with her, "why'd you really pull the whole family dinner thing tonight?"

"Family dinners are more fun, don't you think?"

"I think you haven't had dinner with the right guy if that's what you think."

She was definitely not used to this. Marie had practically offered Gina to him on a silver platter and he didn't seem the least bit interested. But that couldn't be right. *All* men were interested in Gina. She was bright and perky and pretty and dainty and everything else men liked.

Marie was a *mechanic,* for Pete's sake.

Female mechanics weren't exactly the stuff of men's fantasies. She climbed up another step.

How many stairs are there here, anyway? Shouldn't she be near the top? She didn't want to take her eyes off Davis long enough to check. She had the distinct feeling that he'd been militarily trained to take advantage of an opponent's momentary lapses.

Just as that thought whipped through her mind, she reached the second-story landing. Her own little porch, where two pots of dead geraniums decorated her doorway. The last frost had killed them off and she hadn't had time to replace them yet. Stupid, she told herself. This is no time to be thinking about flowers.

With her free hand, she dug into her purse to find her keys. Naturally they hid from her. She had nowhere else to go. She couldn't back up another step, unless she decided to jump over the railing to the driveway below, and that seemed just a tad excessive.

Talk, she told herself. Say something. *Anything.*

"We're here," she announced as if he hadn't figured that out for himself. "So...thanks again."

He still didn't let go of her hand. Instead he pulled her closer to him. Close enough that she felt as though *she* was wearing the aftershave whose scent was doing such odd things to her knees.

He lifted his free hand to cup her face, and she felt the distinct imprint of each of his fingers on her skin. Not a good sign. Breathe, Marie. Breathe. He tipped her face up until she was staring directly into his eyes. In the muted light, she saw determination glinting in their depths and she knew without a doubt that he was about to kiss her.

"I, uh...don't think this is such a good idea," she whispered, forcing the words past a throat so tight, she could scarcely draw a breath. "I hardly know you."

He smiled and Marie's heartbeat skittered wildly for an instant. "Lady," he said, "I'm a marine. You can trust me."

"Yeah?" she asked on a squeak of sound. "To do what?"

He lowered his head. "Whatever's necessary," he told her just before he slanted his mouth across hers.

Marie gasped, shocked silly by the flood of sensations rippling through her. She'd been kissed before. Not often, but enough to know how to do it without bumping noses or biting lips. But none of the kisses she'd experienced before tonight had prepared her for this.

The earth actually did stand still.

Davis's arms came around her, and as he pressed

her tightly to him, she wound her own arms around his neck. She sighed into his parted lips as her body began a slow meltdown. Then his tongue slipped into her mouth and circled her own in a long, lazy, caress that left her struggling for air and clamoring for more.

Heart pounding, knees wobbling, Marie leaned into him, giving herself up to the sensations rushing through her. And when he finally pulled his head back, breaking that incredible kiss, she was grateful for the strength of his arms still holding her upright.

"So?" he whispered, "how about lunch tomorrow?"

"Sure," she said and knew that if he'd just said *Why don't we fly to the moon tomorrow morning?* she'd have said, "Sure." But how could she be expected to think rationally when she'd just had what could only be described as a monumentally life-shattering moment?

"I'll see you, then," he said, and left her.

She listened to the sound of his footsteps as he went down the stairs. Then alone, she gripped the banister tightly and prayed she'd be able to move before it started raining again.

Things are starting to get interesting, Davis told himself as he parked outside Santini's auto repair shop. Heck, even the sun had decided to shine for a change.

He got out of the car and stood in the street, staring at the little shop that Marie's talent with cars kept going. But he wasn't seeing the garage. Instead he was reliving that kiss on her landing. As he had all last night, he remembered every instant of the time he'd held her close. The pounding of her heart, the taste of her, her soft breath brushing his cheek and the crisp December wind that seemed to envelop them both.

At the first touch of her lips, he'd known this woman was different. Different from every other female he'd ever known before. There was a chemical reaction between them that seemed to linger on in his bloodstream throughout the night.

In that one kiss with Marie, he'd found more than he had expected...and enough to worry him. But not nearly enough to make him back off. He needed to explore what he'd found with her, but he could still keep it simple, he told himself. Keep what they had intimate. He didn't have to get involved with her family.

And on that thought, he started for the open service bay doors. Even on a Sunday she was busy. A testament to her abilities.

As he entered the garage, he heard a muttered "Damn it."

He smiled to himself. Even miracle workers get frustrated, he supposed. "Marie?"

The loud clatter of a metal tool hitting the concrete floor sounded out and a second later, she stepped out from behind the upraised hood of a small Honda. She wore a pair of bib overalls that shouldn't have looked cute, but did, and a tiny white T-shirt. Her hair was pulled back into a ponytail from which one or two strands had escaped to hang on either side of her face. As he watched, she lifted one hand to push the hair out of her way and left a streak of oil behind on her cheek.

"Davis, hi," she said and pulled a shop towel out of her hip pocket. Wiping her hands on the once-white fabric, she walked toward him. "Is it lunch-time already?"

Not exactly the eagerness he'd been hoping for, but at least she hadn't forgotten all about their date.

"Yeah," he said. "You ready?"

"Actually," she told him, with a glance at the Honda, "no."

"No?"

She lifted both hands and shrugged. "Well, a friend of mine dropped her car off this morning and it's an emergency, so I told her I'd fix it right away."

"She could drive it here and it was an emergency?" he asked, sure she was just trying to slip out of their lunch date.

"More like it lurched its way here," Marie told him. "The points and plugs are bad and Laura really needs this car for tomorrow morning."

Disappointment rose up inside him, but he pushed it away. It was just lunch, right? "What about one of your loaners?" he asked, and turned to where the three junkers were usually parked.

They weren't there.

"Well, see," Marie said, "that's the problem. I've already loaned them out."

Okay, now he was confused. Loaners were sup-posed to be for her customers' use. But the Honda was the only car at the shop. Curious, he asked, "Who'd you loan them to?"

She shoved the rag back into her pocket, then tucked both of her hands behind the bib front of her overalls. Rocking back and forth on her heels, she said, "Well, Tommy needed a car to get to band practice...."

"The kid who works for you."

"Yes." She gave him a smile, as if proud he'd remembered. "And Margaret Sanders, a friend of my mom's, needed a car to get to her daughter's house, because her daughter just had twins and Margaret had to be there."

"Well, sure." Why Margaret couldn't have gotten there on her own was beyond him, though.

Marie just looked at him. "And the third one is halfway to San Diego by now. Angela needed to go pick up Jeremy's Christmas present."

"In San Diego?"

"All the stores around here were sold out." She cocked her head to one side. "Do you have any idea how fast video games sell out in stores? It's amazing."

He'd take her word for it. Since he'd never had to do Christmas shopping for anyone, he had no idea what sold and what didn't. Looking at the Honda, he asked, "So how long before you have it up and running?"

Marie followed his gaze and sighed. "At least another hour."

"I'll wait."

She whipped around to look at him, then let her

gaze slide to the closed door between the garage and the office. "There's something else, too," she said. "Last night, when you asked me, I forgot about—"

The closed door opened and Jeremy came through, his eyes widening when he caught sight of Davis.

"Hi! Are you coming with us?" the boy asked.

"Us?" Davis repeated, looking from the kid to Marie.

She shrugged again and smiled.

"To see Santa," Jeremy said. "Well, not the real Santa, but the one at the mall. His helper."

"Santa?" Davis repeated before he could stop himself.

Jeremy grinned. "Some of my friends say there's no Santa, but I figure what if there is and he gets really mad 'cause nobody believes in him? Then maybe he won't bring me the presents I want, so I don't want to make him mad just in case, you know?"

"Yeah." Davis looked away from the boy, idly wondering if all kids talked that much and that fast, or if it was something in the Santini blood. Meeting Marie's eyes, he said, "So after Laura's car, it's Santa?"

"Sorry," she said, "but I promised."

"And a promise is a promise, huh, Marie?" Jeremy sounded like he was gloating.

Davis started thinking. Damn it, he wasn't going to lose out to a tune-up and a visit to Santa. He'd been wanting to get Marie all to himself for several days now and he figured with a bit of finagling, he could still manage it.

"How about," he offered, walking to Marie's side, "if I do the tune-up on this heap while you take Jeremy to see Santa? I'll be finished by the time you get back and then we can drop him off at home and go to lunch." Not bad at all, he told himself. A solution worthy of Solomon.

"Nope."

He was getting very little appreciation for his brilliance.

"What do you mean, no?" he asked. "I know as much about cars as you do."

"Maybe," she said, "but this is my shop. I work on the cars here. It's my reputation, my responsibility."

"Okay, I can understand that," he said. He didn't want to, but he did. "But there's got to be a way to work this out."

From the corner of his eye, he saw Jeremy watching them and he half wondered if she'd planned this, too. Like last night's family dinner. Was she deliberately trying to avoid being alone with him?

After a long minute, she offered, "There is one way...if you're up to it."

He responded to the implied dare like any true Devil Dog. "Lady, I keep telling you. I'm a marine. We're up to anything."

"All right, then," she said, "you take Jeremy to the mall to see Santa. And as soon as I'm finished here, I'll meet you in Santa's Village."

"Now, wait a minute," he said loud enough to

be heard over Jeremy's shouts. "There's got to be another way. I'll go to your house. Pick up Gina. She could—"

"Gina's at a ballroom dance class."

"Your mother…"

"Is getting her hair done."

"Angela…"

"San Diego," she reminded him.

Why, Davis wondered, did he suddenly feel like he was being surrounded by heavily armored tanks?

"This is the only way, Davis," Marie said.

He glanced at the boy waiting for his decision. Well, hell. He had two choices here. Charge or retreat. Like any good marine, he made his decisions quickly.

"All right."

Jeremy shouted again and raced out of the garage toward Davis's car.

A mall. On a weekend. At Christmastime.

Davis had gone into battle feeling more confident of his chances for survival.

"One hour," Marie said, breaking into his thoughts. "Outside Santa's Workshop."

Santa's Workshop.

Ooh-rah.

Six

The parking lot was like a battlefield.

The only difference was there were no sides here. It was every man—and woman—for himself. Davis gripped the steering wheel tight enough to snap it in two and tried to keep his eyes on everything at once. Heck, his military training actually helped here. Watch for your chance to advance and protect your flanks.

"We're gonna be late," Jeremy whined from the passenger seat beside him.

"Don't worry, kid," Davis said, "I'm never late."

A woman in a red BMW convertible with a holly wreath attached to her front grille, cut him off, then flipped him a hand gesture substantially lacking in holiday spirit. Gritting his teeth, Davis decided to quit trying to get close to the actual mall and settled instead for a parking space that looked to be miles from the shopping center.

At least they were out of the fray.

He shut the engine off and looked at the boy. Jeremy practically vibrated with excitement. No matter if he denied it or not, the kid obviously placed high faith in Santa Claus. He looked down into those shining eyes and knew without a doubt that *this* kid's Christmas dreams would come true. The Santini women would see to it. This child wouldn't know the disappointment of a Christmas morning with nothing to show for it.

Memories swelled inside him, and Davis fought them back valiantly. The past had no more power over him, he reminded himself. He'd come a long way from the boy he'd been. From the boy who'd learned early that to believe in people was to set yourself up for a letdown.

"Can we go now?" Jeremy asked, unhooking his seat belt and reaching for the door handle.

"Yeah," Davis said, suddenly wanting to hurry up and get this whole Santa thing behind him. "Let's go."

He got out, locked up the car and came around the back end where Jeremy stood waiting for him. As they started for the mall, the boy slid his hand into Davis's and started tugging, trying to make him hurry.

Glancing down at the kid, Davis felt warmed by the small hand in his. He'd never been around children much and when he had, he'd deliberately kept his distance. But lately it seemed distance was the one thing he couldn't seem to maintain.

"Christmas is almost here, y'know," Jeremy said, and anticipation colored his voice.

Doing a quick mental count, Davis told him, "There's still nearly three weeks to go."

"But it's *almost* here."

Apparently everyone agreed with the boy. Even on base, the holiday season was in full swing. Most of his friends had already scheduled leaves to be with their families, and those that were remaining on base were planning celebrations. Davis, though, couldn't even remember a time when Christmas wasn't just a hard time to get through.

Not that he had anything against Christmas. Or Easter. Or Hanukkah. Or the Fourth of July. But all of those things meant family. The one thing Davis had never known. The succession of foster homes he'd moved through as a child hadn't been more than places to sleep—and to escape from. Maybe there were *good* foster homes out there, but he'd never been in one.

As soon as he was old enough, he'd joined the corps and found his place in the world. It had been more than enough for too many years to count. And that place was still his, right?

"What do you want for Christmas, Davis?"

"Huh?" His mind had wandered and he came back now with a jolt as a VW sailed past them. He'd better pay attention or they'd both get run down by holiday maniacs.

"For Christmas," Jeremy repeated. "What do you want?"

"Oh," he said, then shrugged. Instantly, visions of Marie, wrapped up in a red ribbon and not much else rose up in his mind. But since he could hardly say so to her nephew, he said only, "Nothing."

The boy laughed and shook his head. "Everybody wants something."

Wanting and getting are two very different things. And a part of Davis hoped the boy never found that out. Changing the subject slightly, he asked, "What does your aunt Marie want? Do you know?"

Jeremy grinned and tugged a little harder on Davis's hand. It still looked as though the mall was miles in the distance.

"I'm getting her a new wrench," the boy said proudly.

Davis smiled. "She'll like that."

"I know," Jeremy said, obviously sure of himself. "Gina says Santa should bring Marie a man."

Davis's eyebrows lifted.

"But my mom says Marie wouldn't know what to do with one anyway."

Remembering that kiss in the dark, Davis thought he'd have to argue Angela's point. Still, it did him good to know that there weren't other men in Marie's life. That thought sobered him for a minute. He wasn't *in* her life. Was he?

"Marie doesn't have boyfriends?" he asked, allowing himself to be pulled along in the boy's wake.

Jeremy laughed and shook his head. "No way," he said. "She's not like Gina."

True, Davis thought. And for himself, he was grateful for the differences. But he wanted to hear what the kid had to say, so he prodded him a little. "What do you mean?"

"Marie does neat stuff," Jeremy said. "Like fishing and baseball. She doesn't have time to go on dates."

That was certainly true. Davis had never had to work so hard to try and get a woman alone.

"Are *you* gonna be her boyfriend?" Jeremy asked suddenly.

Davis looked down at the kid. The boy watched him warily, waiting for his answer. When it came, it was another question. "Do you think I should be?"

Jeremy stopped dead, tilted his head to one side and thought about it for a long moment. Finally he said, "Yeah. 'Cause you could teach me how to hit really good, and I think Marie kinda likes you."

"You do, huh?" he asked, surprised at the jolt of warmth that rushed through him at the idea. "Why?"

"'Cause she acts kinda funny when you're around. Like she's breathin' weird or something."

Last night stormed into the front of his mind again and he remembered her rapid heartbeat and the brush of her breath against his cheek. They'd both been breathing weird then.

"So I think you should, okay?"

Davis looked at the kid and smiled. "I'll do my best," he said, and had every intention of keeping that promise. He wouldn't mind being Marie's boyfriend at all. At least, temporarily.

Kids.

Millions of them screamed and laughed and cried and jumped up and down in excitement. The line leading around Santa's Workshop, through the Village and up to the throne where the big man sat, crawled forward at a snail's pace. Davis shifted from foot to foot, held Jeremy back from climbing the decorative fence that separated them from the artificial snow and wondered wildly how he'd let himself get talked into this.

The whole place was nuts. The kids around him were worked up to a fever pitch and the Christmas carols coming in over the loudspeaker had repeated themselves three times. And yet, despite everything, a part of him had enjoyed it all.

Finally an elf escorted Jeremy to the throne and the boy took his seat on Santa's lap. While the two of them talked, another elf snapped a picture and turned to Davis with a smile.

"Would you like a picture of your son with Santa?" she asked, giving him a slow look up and down. "Only four dollars."

"He's not—" Davis broke off before he could deny fatherhood. This elf didn't know or care who he and Jeremy were. And for some odd reason, as he stood there, surrounded by children and their parents, he actually *wanted* to belong. To be a part of this madness.

For the first time in his life, he felt close to the

joy that other people took for granted. He turned his gaze to Jeremy and watched as the child told all his secrets to a man in a Santa suit, and he found himself hoping that the kid would never be disappointed. He wanted to think that the boy would always feel the magic that he felt now. That he would never lose the happiness that wreathed his face.

"Sir?" the elf said. "The picture?"

Davis shifted his gaze from the pretty young elf to the boy still whispering secretively to Santa. His heart swelled suddenly. He didn't stop to question the unusual emotions taking hold of him. He didn't want to examine them too closely.

"Yeah," Davis told her, his gaze still fixed on Jeremy. "I'll take it." He reached for his wallet to buy a little piece of Christmas.

Marie hurried through the mall, dodging harried shoppers laden down with overflowing bags. The tune-up had taken longer than she'd thought and then she'd had to go home and change clothes. Even she refused to go to the shopping center covered in motor oil and grease.

Hurrying her steps toward the center of the mall, she ran the flat of one hand down the front of her beige sweater and stopped atop her nervous stomach. Most people got butterflies when they were nervous. She felt as though bats were flying around inside her.

The crowd of kids was still thick around Santa's Village and her gaze scanned the mob, looking for two familiar faces. They weren't there, though, so she turned to look at the surrounding stores and finally spotted them sitting at a café opposite the Workshop.

Her heartbeat staggered and her mouth went dry. Even across a crowded mall, he had the ability to destroy her equilibrium. Mind spinning, she wondered how it had happened that in less than a week she'd become so...involved with this man? It had been years since she'd indulged in the kind of dreams that had haunted her sleep last night, and that fact worried her as much as it excited her.

Mainly because Marie still didn't know why he appeared to be so interested in her. But she was beginning to enjoy it. And a part of her was already dreading the day he'd move on in search of a more female female.

Surely soon, the novelty of chasing after a woman mechanic would wear off. Then he'd quit coming around—or worse yet, start treating her like a pal. Something cold and tight squeezed around her heart and Marie almost winced at the sensation. She didn't need or want another "buddy."

But darned if she didn't want him.

Gathering what was left of her unraveling self-control, she hurried through the crowd separating them.

"Hi," she said as she slid into a seat beside Jeremy.

Davis's gaze locked on to hers and she felt a slow heat climbing inside her. So much for self-control.

"I already talked to Santa, Marie," Jeremy said, "and Davis bought a picture of me so you could see it.'' He handed her the photo and added in a whisper, ''But don't show it to anybody except Mom and Grandma, okay?''

''Okay,'' she told him, and hardly glanced at the picture before looking at Davis again. ''Thanks. Thanks for bringing him and for this.''

''No problem,'' he told her. ''Get the tune-up finished?''

Good, she thought. Safe ground. ''Yeah. But the car's nearly done for. I don't know if I can keep it running much longer.''

''How come Laura doesn't buy a new car?'' Jeremy piped up.

''She can't afford to, honey,'' Marie said.

''Maybe Santa will bring her one.''

''Maybe.'' But Santa didn't usually take adults' dreams and wishes to heart. Maybe he figured adults were capable of making their own dreams come true. And speaking of dreams...

Marie couldn't seem to tear her gaze from Davis's. Ever since last night, she'd been thinking about him, reliving that kiss and warning herself not to pump up her balloon to the bursting point. A kiss that had curled her toes didn't necessarily mean the same thing to him. Maybe he hadn't felt the same connection she had.

But now, staring into his blue eyes, she had the decided impression that he, too, was remembering those few minutes in the darkness.

''How about we take Jeremy home and go for an early dinner?'' he asked suddenly, and she wondered

if his voice had really dropped a couple of notches
or if she was just imagining it.

Dinner. She thought about it for a long second or
two, then decided yes, she'd go to dinner with him.
Once they had a little time alone, he'd see she
wasn't his type and go away. Hopefully before she
got hurt too badly. Besides, she wanted to be with
him again, if only for the last time. She wanted to
be kissed again. She wanted to feel the heat rising
within her. To feel his arms wrapped around her.
For once in her life, she wanted to know what it felt
like to be *wanted* by a man. By this man. And she
had to do it quickly, before he came to his senses.

"Okay," she said simply and hoped he hadn't
heard the slight tremor in her voice.

"Hey," Jeremy complained, "I'm hungry, too."

One of Davis's eyebrows lifted in a silent question.

She answered him by speaking to her nephew.
"Not tonight, kiddo." Her gaze slid back to Davis's
as she added, "Tonight is for grown-ups."

"Lord, girl," Gina exclaimed, "don't you *ever*
condition your hair?"

"Of course I do," Marie said, then yelped,
"Ow!" when her little sister dragged a brush
through the tangled curls.

She glared into the mirror at Gina's reflection and
when her sister was unmoved, shifted that glare to
the other two women encamped in her bedroom.

Since finding out about Marie's dinner date, the
three of them had pulled out all the stops. Appar-

ently they were bound and determined to push Marie through the doors of femininity, kicking and screaming if need be.

Her bedroom, her sanctuary, looked like a bomb had gone off in it. A mound of dresses that had been tried on and discarded covered the mattress. Shoes, stockings and more makeup than Marie had ever seen before lay strewn across every other possible surface.

Jeremy had been left in the main house to play video games on the TV while the Santini women transformed Marie into—she looked at her own reflection and sighed inwardly—a gorgeous stranger.

Gina yanked the brush through the still-warm curls again and Marie made a grab at her hair. "You don't mind leaving a few strands on my head, do you?"

"Only if they're curled and shining," Gina snapped.

"You have to suffer for beauty," Mama said from her perch on the edge of Marie's bed.

"And who made up that rule?" she demanded hotly. "A man?"

"Probably," Angela conceded as she slapped Marie's hand away from the dangerously low-scooped neckline of her borrowed red dress. "And stop tugging on the fabric. It's not going to come up any higher and you'll wrinkle it."

"My boobs will fall out," Marie told her, and laid the flat of her hand atop the swell of her breasts. She'd never worn a dress cut so low and knew that she'd have pneumonia before the end of the night.

Figures that Gina's dress would be cut low enough to display all of her charms.

How had she let herself be talked into wearing the slinky red number? But even as she thought it, she knew the answer. Because just for tonight she wanted to be more than she usually was. Just for tonight she wanted to be the homecoming queen, the prom princess and Miss America all rolled into one.

"Your boobs will *not* fall out," Gina told her with a grin. "But if you're lucky, they may be helped to escape."

"Gina…" Mama's voice sounded stern, but they all knew the woman had long since given up trying to rein in her youngest daughter.

"If they don't freeze and break off before then," Marie whispered.

Angela picked up a tube of lipstick and a tiny brush, then turned Marie's face toward her. "God knows, I hate to agree with Gina on anything, but honestly, Marie, it's high time you did something like this."

"Amen," Gina muttered, and jabbed Marie's skull with a rhinestone barrette.

Marie winced and tried to pull away. Angela's fingers tightened on her chin.

"You're a pretty girl," Mama said. "You should make the most of it."

"By wearing enough paint to hide my identity?" Marie asked, giving a sideways glance into the mirror. Hmm. The rhinestones looked kind of nice the way they held back a wave of curls and twinkled against her dark hair.

"To accentuate your inner beauty," Gina said, making her voice high and pompous.

Inner beauty. Right. What all men were interested in.

Angela finished painting on lipstick and released her chin. Then she studied Marie's face as though it was a just finished work of art. "Good," she said to herself before reaching for the tiny bottle of expensive perfume she'd brought with her.

Leaning forward, she dabbed some of the luxurious scent behind each of Marie's ears, then handed her the crystal stopper. "Touch the scent between your breasts," she ordered.

Marie gripped the crystal tightly enough to snap it. This was getting out of hand, she thought for what had to be the hundredth time since submitting herself to her sisters' care. "Isn't it enough they're exposed to the entire world? Do they have to smell, too?"

"Oh, brother," Gina muttered as she jabbed another rhinestone barrette into place on the other side of Marie's head. "All of this is wasted on you, you know that?"

"That's enough, Gina," Mama told her.

"Well, really," the youngest Santini sister went on, curling some of Marie's hair around her finger and smoothing it into place. "She's Italian, for heaven's sake! Hot-blooded, just like the rest of us."

Oh, Marie thought, her blood was plenty hot and getting hotter every minute.

"Italian doesn't mean sex crazed," Angela chimed in.

"Then it's been so long, you don't remember," Gina snapped.

"All right!" Mama clapped her hands and said, "That's enough now. Marie will be who she is and—" she looked into the mirror to meet her middle daughter's gaze "—that's more than enough for any man."

Marie gave her a soft smile and, touched, whispered, "Thanks, Mama."

The older woman smiled back and lifted one hand to emphasize her next point. "Though that's not to say that a little advertising doesn't hurt. Now put that perfume where your sister told you to. And Gina, I really don't want to know about your hot blood, all right?"

"None of us do," Angela added.

"Jealous," Gina told them. "You're all jealous."

Marie dutifully touched the stopper to the valley between her breasts and shivered at the feel of the cold glass against her heated skin. When she handed the perfume back to her sister, she took a last look at herself in the mirror.

It was her reflection and yet so different.

"Nice, huh?" Gina said, admiring her handiwork.

"Nice nothing," Angela said. "She's gorgeous."

"She always has been," Mama put in.

Marie stared at herself for a long moment, then took a deep breath that swelled her breasts high enough to convince her not to do *that* real often, and stood up. "Okay, I guess I'm as ready as I'll ever be."

"Wait'll Davis gets a load of you," Gina said with a grin.

Angela smiled and reached out to smooth the skirt of Marie's dress. "His eyes'll pop out, honey."

Marie's eyes suddenly stung with the threat of tears. She'd never done this before. Shared a feminine bonding session over makeup and clothes with her sisters and her mother. It felt strange, and...good.

"Don't you *dare* get all weepy and ruin your makeup," Gina warned sternly.

Marie laughed, as she was meant to, and thought maybe they were right. Maybe it was high time for her to come out from under her overalls and take a look at the world through female eyes.

A knock at the door sounded.

And maybe, she thought with a sharp pang of insecurity, it wasn't too late to cancel this whole thing.

"He's here," Gina said unnecessarily.

"Oh, God," Marie whispered through a suddenly tight throat.

"You look wonderful, Marie," Mama said as she crossed the room to hug her. "Now don't worry about a thing. Just be yourself."

Marie knew it was good advice, but how could she be herself when she didn't even look like herself? Nope. That wouldn't work. Tonight she would be someone else. Someone as hot-blooded as Gina. Someone as beautiful as Angela. Someone as confident as Mama.

Tonight she was the best of all the Santini women—and the Marie she'd always secretly yearned to be.

Seven

Davis knocked on the door again and couldn't help wondering if she'd changed her mind again. Maybe she wouldn't go out with him at all. And maybe, he told himself, they'd be accompanied by one of her sisters. Or her mother. Or Jeremy.

He'd never before been involved with a woman so devoted to family. And he still wasn't sure he liked it.

Overhead, a clear winter sky gleamed with millions of stars, and the ever-present ocean wind pushed at him with its cold breath. He stuffed his hands into his trouser pockets and wished his suit coat was warmer.

Then the door opened and every thought in his head, but one...dissolved.

Beautiful. Marie Santini was absolutely the most breathtaking woman he'd ever seen. Backlit by a solitary lamp, her dark hair shone around the glittering clips holding the thick mass back from her face. For the first time since he'd known her, she was wearing makeup, but only enough to emphasize the beauty of her eyes and the lush fullness of her lips. A soft floral scent reached out to him, and he inhaled it greedily as his gaze drifted down and over her. His heart lurched a bit and his breathing quickened as he admired the swell of her breasts above the low neckline of her dress. Long red sleeves encased her slender arms and the short hem of the dress swirled around a pair of amazing legs.

Slowly he lifted his gaze again until he was looking into her green eyes. Then he smiled, shook his head and said, ''Lady, you're incredible.''

She smiled and lifted her chin a bit higher, giving her hair a shake. ''Thank you. Tonight I *feel* incredible.''

And he felt lucky. So damned lucky, he was sure something would go wrong.

''Are you ready?'' he asked, and held out one hand toward her.

''As I'll ever be,'' she said, and picked up her coat from a nearby chair. Then she stepped out onto the porch and closed the door behind her.

That scent of hers enveloped him, and Davis had all he could do to keep from grabbing her and pulling her close. He wanted to taste her mouth again. But they had a dinner reservation to keep. Which was too bad, since the only thing he was hungry for was her.

Small bouquets of holly and poinsettias decorated every table, and in the far corner of the restaurant a fire blazed on the brick-faced hearth. The soft clink of crystal and the hush of muted conversations drifted through the room, but Davis paid no attention to any of it. He only had eyes for Marie.

Unfortunately so did their waiter.

At the thought of him, the man appeared with their dessert, and keeping his fascinated gaze locked on Marie, damn near dumped a slice of apple pie into Davis's lap.

"Hey!" he said, and caught the china plate just in time.

The waiter spared him a fast glance and a less-than-apologetic shrug. "Sorry." Then shifting his gaze back to the object of his affections, he asked, "Would you like more coffee, miss?"

Davis gritted his teeth. He was used to other men admiring his dates. What he wasn't used to was this smattering of anger that churned in his guts every time the waiter drooled on Marie. Jealousy? he wondered, surprised at himself. Hell, he'd never been jealous before and had even laughed at his friends when they described the ugly emotions he was now experiencing. But damn it, there was nothing funny about watching a stranger ogling Marie.

"Coffee?" the waiter asked again, and Davis prepared to scoot out of range.

She gave him a small smile and shook her head, "No, thanks."

As the man walked away, Davis said, "I appreciate your turning down the coffee. Otherwise, I might get third-degree burns in an area I'd rather keep unharmed."

Marie chuckled. "I think he's sweet."

"You would," he said, giving the man's back a hard look. "He didn't dump a salad in your lap."

"At least it was served with dressing on the side," she said on a laugh.

True, he thought. Instead of picking dry lettuce off his slacks, he could have been doused with blue cheese dressing.

"And have you recovered from the waiter's slip?" she asked, laying her forearms on the linen-covered tabletop and leaning forward. Her movement gave him an excellent view of the breasts he'd been trying all evening not to stare at.

Recovered? he thought. Hell, no. He was sinking fast.

"I'll live as long as he doesn't come back with some flaming dessert."

She laughed again and he found himself enjoying the sound.

"This was really nice, Davis," she said, dragging his attention back to her face and the eyes that haunted him. "Thank you for bringing me."

"I've been trying to get you to go out with me since I met you," he reminded her.

"Was it worth the wait?" she asked, a teasing note in her voice.

"Oh," he said with a slight nod, "definitely."

"Good." She picked up a spoon and took a small bite of sherbet. Her lips closed over the icy sweet, and he watched her sigh as the flavors dissolved on her tongue.

He shifted uncomfortably in his seat and was privately grateful that the room was so dimly lit. Otherwise he'd have to keep his suit coat buttoned when they left, to avoid embarrassing himself.

"How long have you been a marine?"

"Hmm?" He shook his head to clear it. "What?"

She grinned at him. "I asked how long you've been a marine."

"Oh." Keep your mind on the conversation, he thought. "Forever."

"That long?" Marie smiled and took another bite of sherbet. "You look pretty good for your advanced age."

And he was aging by the minute, thinking about her and him and what he'd rather they be doing instead of sitting here making polite conversation. "Thanks, I think."

She licked her spoon, and the slow swipe of her tongue did incredible things to his pulse rate.

"So how long really?" she asked.

"Close to fifteen years," he managed to say.

"Are you a lifer?" she asked, dipping that spoon back into the sherbet he was beginning to envy.

"Yeah," he said, tearing his gaze from her mouth and the sensuous way she ate the damned dessert. "Always figured to be in for the long haul."

"Really? There's nothing else you'd want to do?"

For one brief minute, Davis thought about his old dream of opening a car-restoration place. Heck, he had several different cars tucked away in various storage garages across the country. Wherever he was stationed, he'd buy an old junker and slowly restore it himself. He'd always told himself it was a hobby, but the truth was it gave him something to do when he wasn't on duty. A man with no family and ties had too much free time.

He'd never told anyone else about that old dream, but tonight, he found himself telling Marie. When he was finished, she asked, "Why don't you do it? Open your own place, I mean."

"No." Davis shook his head and pushed the slice of apple pie to one side. "I don't know if I could stand staying in one place too long."

"Funny," she mused, and pushed her unfinished sherbet aside. "I don't know that I could move around as much as you do." She shook her head slowly. "A new home every few years? No place to call your own?"

"Root-bound, huh?" he teased.

"And you're rootless," she said softly.

"I guess there's no middle ground between the two, huh?" he asked.

"I don't think so," she said softly.

He reached across the table and covered her hand with his. The quick flash of heat that erupted when they touched warmed him through as he asked,

"Haven't you ever wanted to just...take off? Move somewhere new?"

"Take off?" she repeated.

"Yeah. Go somewhere where no one knows you."

Marie shook her head. "No. Why would I?"

Davis frowned and linked their fingers together. "To be on your own. Alone to do whatever you want."

She smiled at him, but her eyes looked confused. "I already have that."

"Do you?" he asked. "I've known you several days and I almost never see you without Jeremy or Gina or your mom...."

"They're my family," she protested.

She didn't understand, and he knew he shouldn't have expected her to. She hadn't grown up being shuttled from place to place. She hadn't learned early that "he travels fastest who travels alone." There was no way she could possibly know the benefits of having no one to lay claim to your time. Your life.

"Quicksand," he muttered.

"What?"

He inhaled deeply and linked his fingers with hers. Her thumb stroked the back of his hand and a part of his mind concentrated solely on the sensations she was stirring within him.

"Families," he said thickly. "I've always thought of them as quicksand." Explaining, he went on. "Stay too close and they suck you in and then under. You're trapped. Never free to be whoever you might want to be.''

Marie watched him and tried to read his expression, but it seemed Davis Garvey had had too many years to learn to hide what he was thinking. She couldn't understand his feelings about family and thought his way seemed a lonely way to live.

Instantly images of her family rose up in her mind and she knew that without them, her life would be an empty thing.

''I've always thought of my family as a lifeboat,'' she said quietly, trying to ease the shadow of old pain from his eyes.

''What do you mean?''

''You know,'' she said, continuing to stroke the back of his hand with her thumb, ''a safety net, sort of. Where each of us is there to help the other. To back each other up in times of trouble and to cheer for each other when things are great. Mama says that home is a place that, when you go there, they have to let you in.''

He didn't say anything and Marie asked quietly, ''Where's your safety net, Davis?''

He gave her hand a squeeze, then released her and reached for the leather folder that held their bill. Giving her a smile that didn't quite hide the shadows still lurking in his eyes, he said, ''I guess right now it's Camp Pendleton.''

As he glanced at the bill and counted out the appropriate amount of money, she asked, ''I know you said you don't have a family. But surely there's someone?''

"Just the corps," he said, then must have noticed the sympathy in her eyes. "Don't bother feeling sorry for me," he said with a half smile. "Quicksand, remember?"

"Yes," she said, "I remember." But she couldn't help wondering if he'd still feel that way if there was a family standing beside him.

She'd seen his patience and kindness with Jeremy and his friendliness toward her sisters and her mother. Marie had a feeling that Davis Garvey didn't even realize how starved for family he really was. This was a man who'd obviously spent so much of his life alone, he'd come to believe that it was the only way to live.

Her heart ached just a little for the man who had so much to give and no one to give it to.

While Davis settled their bill, Marie waited on the wooden deck that stretched along behind the row of restaurants lining the harbor. The cold, sea-kissed breeze whipped around her, sending her skirt hem into a wild dance around her thighs.

She tipped her face into the wind and felt the sting of salt air caress her cheeks and chest with dampness. With her earlier worries about pneumonia banished along with the rest of her rational mind, she let her coat hang open so that the wind could wrap itself around her.

"You must be freezing," Davis said as he came up behind her.

Startled, she turned to look at him, and in the soft glow of the deck lights, she saw his eyes darken as he stared at her. Maybe a part of her should be offended that he was so obviously attracted to the "new and improved" Marie—the stranger she was tonight. But watching his eyes as he watched her sent spirals of heat unwinding throughout her body. A slow, deep ache settled low in her belly, and it felt as though an iron band was wrapped tightly around her chest, making it difficult to breathe.

He draped one arm around her shoulders and pulled her close to him. Her back to his front, she felt the hard, solid strength of him, and a skittering of heat dazzled her bloodstream. This was something elemental. A powerful connection lay between them and this was the night Marie had decided to explore it. To discover what she'd always dreamed of discovering. To find in Davis's arms the magic she knew other women had found.

His arms came around her and they stood, staring out at the harbor. The luxury homes across the water sparkled with thousands of twinkling Christmas lights. Reflections of those lights shone on the black water, looking as though handfuls of multicolored stars had fallen from the sky.

From somewhere far off, the muted strains of "Silent Night" drifted toward them. Marie's breath caught in her throat. It was all so beautiful. So perfect.

He held her tighter and she shivered.

"You *are* cold," he whispered close to her ear, and the brush of his warm breath on her flesh made her tremble.

Cold? She didn't think she'd ever be cold again. Not with the fires blazing inside her.

"No," she whispered with a shake of her head, "I'm not cold. I'm..."

"What?" He turned her in his arms and held her tightly, pressing her body into his.

Looking down into her eyes, he captured her gaze and held it until Marie thought she might drown in the crystal-blue depths that held so many secrets and so much warmth.

How could it be possible she'd known him only a few days? At that moment, she felt as though she'd always known him. That a part of her had always been waiting for him. And it didn't matter anymore that he would leave her one day. All that mattered now was that tonight, for now, he was hers. And she suddenly wanted to be his.

"Marie?" he asked, and lifted one hand to smooth his fingertips along her cheek.

She swallowed heavily and closed her eyes briefly at the sensation of warmth trickling from his fingers into her soul. Looking at him again, she said only, "Kiss me, Davis."

"My pleasure," he whispered, and bent his head to claim her mouth.

Gently at first, his lips met hers. Softly, tenderly, he kissed her as the wind raced around them, binding them together in an icy embrace. Then he cupped her cheek with his palm and deepened that kiss, entering her mouth when she sighed, his tongue caressing her warmth, stealing her breath.

Marie's heartbeat raced, her stomach flip-flopped

and her knees wobbled. She leaned into him, trusting him to hold her upright as her world spun. It was everything their last kiss had been and more. So much more that Marie didn't want it to stop. She didn't want these sensations to end. And when he lifted his head to look at her, she looked deeply into his eyes and said, "Let's go home, Davis."

She knew he heard the need quivering in her voice and saw the desire shining in her eyes. "Are you sure?" he asked.

Marie inhaled deeply, drawing the scent of him deep inside her. She would never be able to catch a whiff of Old Spice again without remembering this moment in the Christmas-lit darkness with him. Every nerve tingled with anticipation. Every sense strained to the breaking point. Her breath hitched, her stomach rolled and that ache low in her body seemed to throb in time with her pulse beat.

Sure? Dear heaven, if he didn't get her home quickly, the new and improved Marie was going to toss him to the wooden deck and have her way with him. And the mental images inspired by *that* notion nearly pushed her over the precarious precipice on which she felt balanced.

Mouth dry, heart pounding, she lifted her hands to the lapels of his coat and hung on. Then tipping her head back to look at him squarely, she whispered harshly, "Davis, trust me on this. I'm *very* sure."

He groaned tightly, pulled in a long, deep breath, then winked at her. "Me, too."

Eight

Okay, she *had* been sure.

On the deck, on their hurried walk to the parking lot, for most of the drive home. But, as the silence in the car thickened, her nerve had started slipping.

What was she doing?

She wasn't a one-night-stand kind of girl.

For pity's sake, was she out of her mind?

Davis parked the car in the driveway and Marie tossed a quick glance at the main house. Why did she suddenly feel like a hormone-enraged teenager sneaking around with her boyfriend? She was a grown woman. Twenty-six years old and about to finally lose the humiliating fact of her virginity.

She choked back an hysterical laugh.

Sure. Nothing to be nervous about.

"Marie?" Davis asked, and she lifted her gaze to his. In the dim light, she saw his concern warring with the desire still thumping through her despite a sudden rush of doubts. "Are you okay?"

"Yeah," she muttered, and groped blindly for the door handle. "Dandy." She got out of the car and started walking toward the stairs leading to her apartment. Every click of her heels against the cement seemed to be echoing a message. Unfortunately it was a very confusing message. At first she heard, *Do it, do it.* And in the next instant, she imagined a voice shouting, *Stop this, stop this.*

Oh, great. Even her conscience was muddled.

Just when she needed to be able to think straight, her brain was a jumble of wants and desires and warnings and guilt pangs. But what did she have to be guilty about?

She lifted one hand to her forehead as she started up the stairs. Hearing Davis only a step or two behind her did nothing to calm the frenzy roaring through her.

At the landing, she dug out her house key, slid it into the lock and turned it. Before she could step inside, though, Davis's hand on her arm stopped her.

"Hey," he said quietly, and his breath misted before him in the cold. "I don't know what's going on in that mind of yours, but—"

"It's nothing," she said quickly, fighting down her nerves. She'd come this far. She didn't want to quit now, did she?

A single lamp had been left burning in the apartment and a fragile slice of light framed the two of them as they stood there, staring at each other.

"It's something," Davis said, and laid both hands on her shoulders. "Marie, we don't have to do this. If you've changed your mind—" he forced a strained laugh "—I'll just crawl back to my car and limp back to the base."

A groan squeezed from her throat and Marie rested her forehead on his chest. She felt the pounding of his heart and knew the frantic beat matched her own. If he left now, he wouldn't be the only one crawling to safety. She wanted him so badly, her whole body seemed to be crying out for the feel of him. So why was she hesitating now when before it had felt so right?

Lifting her head, she looked at him and whispered, "Davis, I don't know *what* I want...."

One corner of his mouth tilted into a half smile and he shrugged. "Then we wait."

"But I don't—"

"Shh..." He laid one finger across her mouth and a splinter of warmth touched her. "It's okay."

"No, it's not." Disgusted with herself, Marie stepped back from him, halfway through the doorway and tossed her purse into the apartment. When she looked back at him, he was smiling. "What?"

"That." He pointed over her head to the tiny green plant nailed to the door frame. A red ribbon dangled from its leaves and Marie knew darn well the plant hadn't been there when she left.

Gina.

She didn't know if she wanted to throttle her sister or thank her.

"It's mistletoe," he said unnecessarily, and took a step closer.

"So it is," she whispered, and felt her body light up again in anticipation.

"Then before I leave, I think we'd better kiss," he said, stepping into the doorway to join her. "Don't want to buck a tradition as old as mistletoe. Who knows what might happen?"

She nodded jerkily. "No point in taking chances."

"Exactly," he whispered, and pulled her into the circle of his arms.

When their lips met, Marie felt it again. That flash of heat and sense of rightness. This is what she'd been missing. On the deck, when he was kissing her, she'd known instinctively that tonight was the night. It was only on the drive home, when she'd had too much time to think, that she'd started doubting her own decision.

She should have known better. This wasn't a time for thinking. This was a time for feeling. Experiencing. For letting go of everything else and grabbing hold of what was being offered. A chance to find a little Christmas magic all her own.

Parting her lips for his tongue, she welcomed him inside and gasped at the intimate caress. Her nerve endings felt frazzled. The pounding of her own heart was deafening. Swirls of want and need and pure, unadulterated lust swam in the pit of her stomach.

This time, when he broke their kiss, Marie didn't let go of him.

Instead she curled her arms around his neck, met his gaze with her own and whispered brokenly, "Make love to me, Davis. Now."

"Marie…" He looked haggard, pushed to the breaking point, and yet there was a gleam of uncertainty in his eyes. As if he was waiting for her to change her mind again.

"I mean it," she said, moving one hand to cup his cheek.

He turned his face into her touch and kissed the center of her palm, tracing the tip of his tongue along her skin until she was shuddering in his grasp.

"I want you," he whispered, and his breath came warm against her flesh.

"I want you right back," she said in a hush. "Now, Davis. For heaven's sake, please, now."

Apparently he saw the truth in her eyes, because he picked her up, stepped into the apartment and kicked the door closed behind him. Nestled in his strong arms, Marie tugged at his knotted tie and when it was free, unbuttoned the top two buttons of his shirt as he walked blindly across the small living room to the couch.

He set her down on her feet and she slipped out of her coat as he did the same. Gazes locked, the only illumination the one small lamp in the far corner, they faced each other and hurriedly yanked at their clothes.

Marie reached behind her to undo the zipper on her borrowed dress and groaned aloud when the blasted thing stuck. Davis came to her side, turned her around and worked it loose, skimming the backs of his knuckles along her spine as he slid the zipper down the length of her back.

"Ohhh..." Marie sighed heavily at the contact, and when he turned her back around to face him, leaned into him, loving the feel of his bare chest and back. She ran her hands up and down his muscular back and pressed herself close to him. And even through the material of his slacks, she felt the hard, rigid proof of his desire straining against her abdomen.

"Davis," she whispered, leaning back in his arms to look up at him, "I need..." How was she supposed to ask for what she needed when she wasn't completely sure herself?

"I need you, too, babe," he said, and began to drag his mouth along the line of her throat and down to her chest and the swell of her bosom. And then he stopped one last time. "No more doubts?" he asked quietly.

"None," she told him, more sure of this than anything before in her life.

He nodded and continued on his exploration. "I've been thinking about your breasts all night," he whispered, brushing his breath against her already-heated flesh.

"You have?" she said on a sigh, and felt his talented fingers flick her bra strap open in a single move.

The delicate lace came away in an instant and Davis tossed it to the floor. Before she could even think about embarrassment or anything else for that matter, he lowered her to the couch, cupped her breasts in his palms and bent his head to taste one erect nipple and then the other.

What was left of her brain dissolved into a puddle.

"Oh, my," she said. Mouth dry, eyes wide, she stared up at the ceiling as Davis's lips and teeth did incredible things to her body. Her back arched when he pulled one nipple into his mouth and suckled her. A drawing sensation started in the pit of her stomach and radiated outward until she felt as though he was pulling her soul into his. And just when she thought she would die from the pleasure, he abandoned that breast for the other. Again she felt his lips tug at her as the edges of his teeth nipped and teased her so sensitive skin.

"Davis," she said softly, her hands groping for him. She held the back of his head, pressing him to her so that she could keep him there and continue feeling the amazing sensations rocking her world.

He groaned tightly, and as he suckled her, his fingers toyed with her other nipple until she felt as though she was being pulled in four directions at once. As taut as a wire, her body ached and burned like nothing she'd ever experienced before.

And then it was over and he was sliding down along her body, trailing damp, warm kisses across her rib cage, her abdomen and...lower.

"Davis, do you think...?" She half sat up on the couch and watched through wide eyes as he pulled her black bikini panties down her legs then tossed them to the floor as he had her bra.

Excitement warred with awkward discomfort as she looked at herself to find she was stretched out on her sofa wearing nothing but a pair of black thigh-high stockings. Then her gaze locked with Davis's heated stare and as he watched her, she felt moisture pool at her center. Her flesh seemed to be simmering, her blood boiling, and as he leaned back and scooped her bottom off the couch, even her hair caught fire.

His strong fingers kneaded her tender flesh as he looked at her and Marie couldn't look away from his eyes. The blue depths looked silver in the half-light and they seemed to gleam with an inner blaze that burned as brightly as the flames consuming her.

He lifted her higher off the couch and inched closer to her. She licked her lips and tried to steady her breathing enough to allow air into lungs that felt starved for nourishment.

"Davis, what are you—" She broke off as he bent his head close to the juncture of her thighs. Her leg muscles contracted and she tried to pull free. She hadn't counted on *this*. She'd expected—no *wanted* sex. But this, this was something else again, and she wasn't at all sure that she could let him—

His mouth came down on her and she groaned aloud. Her hips bucked in his hands and she only half felt him ease her legs across his shoulders. She was flying. No longer tethered to the earth, the only hold on reality existed in the touch of Davis's hands on her bottom and the feel of his mouth on her— oh, good heavens!

Her head twisted from side to side on the sofa

cushion. She arched into him and tried to concentrate on every sensation he offered her. His tongue swirled delicately over the tender folds of skin and teased an especially sensitive button of flesh. Marie jerked in his grasp as a lightning-like flash of pure, undiluted pleasure rocketed through her. He did it again, and another jagged bolt, stronger than the first, grabbed at her.

She gave herself up to him, leaving modesty, awkwardness and shyness behind. She tried to part her legs wider, inviting him closer, deeper. Marie sighed when his tongue swept into her depths and groaned when his mouth closed over that one small area that seemed to hold every sensation in the universe.

She rocked against him, her hands reaching for him, her eyes still locked on the ceiling as she felt something hot and dark coil within her. The feeling built and built, feeding on itself, feeding on the pleasure only Davis could bring her. Every cell in her body tightened. Something was there. Just beyond her reach. Hovering, waiting for her to discover its treasures. Her mind blanked to everything but this silent, hungry quest.

She turned her head to look at him and her heart somersaulted in her chest. So intimate. So close. He touched her as no other man ever had and as she wanted no other man to do. Marie felt the strength in his hands and knew that he would keep her safe. Hold her, guide her to the end of this road he was propelling her along.

His tongue swept over that one certain spot again

and she caught a scream and swallowed it as she hurtled toward oblivion. And when the first, glorious shake of completion rattled through her, she rode its wave, secure in his grasp, and let the tiny explosions shatter what was left of her composure.

Moments…maybe hours later, she heard his voice whispering in her ear.

"Come with me, Marie."

Her body still trembling, she opened her eyes to look at him, and when he helped her to her feet, she went with him, leaning against him as he headed for her bedroom.

Outside the window, she could see the strand of Christmas lights twinkling in the darkness. Moonlight slanted through the panes, falling across her double bed as if to point the way toward heaven.

Davis stopped beside the bed, grabbed the comforter and tossed it to the foot of the mattress. Then he eased himself down onto the clean sheets and drew her with him, laying alongside her, holding her tight.

His own heart pounding, he levered himself up on one elbow and looked down into her incredible face. Her hair tumbled about her cheeks. One rhinestone clip was missing and the other clung tenaciously to a single strand of hair.

Gently he disentangled it and set it down on the bedside table. Then he indulged himself. Running his hand across her body, he luxuriated in the soft, smooth feel of her. She sighed and turned toward him. Opening her eyes, she looked up at him and said, "That was amazing, Davis. Absolutely amazing."

Oh, he knew that. He'd felt her climax as surely as if it had been his own. Just the memory of her wild, untamed response to him was enough to make him hard and ready. The taste of her, the feel of her in his hands, was more than he'd ever expected to find. Never before had he felt this kind of...connection to a woman. And that thought both terrified and intrigued him.

But there would be time enough later to think. Now all he wanted was to become a part of her. To claim her body fully with his own. Slipping off the bed, he quickly got rid of the rest of his clothes. And when he lay back down, she opened her arms to him and Davis had the strangest sensation of *coming home*. Looking down into the liquid darkness of her eyes, he felt himself falling—into what, he wasn't sure.

He banished that thought and all others though, a moment later. Her hands moved on his body with a featherlight touch. Tender, gentle, yet demanding. Apparently, she, too, felt the same driving force to join. To couple their bodies and to feel the world drop away.

He bent to her breasts and kissed their soft brown tips again. She arched into him and he smiled against her skin. This they shared. The hunger, the joy.

His left hand dropped lower, crossing her abdomen to the small triangle of curls at the juncture of her thighs. She took a breath, held it and released it in a heavy sigh when his fingertips explored her depths.

A groan built inside him and Davis fought it back. He touched her, stroking her silky body, finding everything he'd ever searched for within her. He dipped one finger, then two inside her. She lifted her hips into his touch and Davis shifted, giving in to the urge to hurry. To enter her. He couldn't wait another minute. Pulse pounding, heart racing, he moved to position himself between her legs.

Then he looked down into her eyes and kept her gaze locked with his as he eased himself in.

Her big green eyes widened farther at his intrusion and he paused, aching to hurry but suddenly needing to go slow. So tight, so warm. He inched farther into her heat and felt her body welcome him, closing around him in a soft grasp.

"Marie," he said on a choked-off groan, and leaned over her, bracing his weight on his hands at either side of her head.

"Come inside me, Davis," she whispered, and licked her lips just to torture him further. "I need to feel you inside me."

He needed that, too. More than his next breath.

Bending his head to hers, he took her mouth in a hard kiss and pushed himself the rest of the way in. She gasped aloud and held perfectly still for a moment. And in that instant, Davis knew what he should have suspected all along.

Her nervousness. Her heated response. Her tight warmth.

Marie Santini was a virgin.

At least she *had* been.

Marie's head tipped back into the pillow and she smiled at the glorious feeling of Davis *inside* her. It was like nothing she'd ever known before. Everything she'd heard, everything she'd read, couldn't have prepared her for the simple *rightness* of it all.

Bodies joined, hearts beating in unison, the power, the magic of it swamped her, leaving her breathless. She looked up into Davis's surprised gaze and knew in that heart-stopping moment that she loved him. As ridiculous as it might sound, she loved a man she'd known less than a week.

And even as logic cried out that it was impossible, her heart knew the truth. It didn't matter if a week or a year had passed. When you found the one person meant for you, the feelings were real. Undeniable. She opened her mouth to say the words she'd always wanted to utter, but Davis spoke before she had the chance.

"Why didn't you tell me?" he ground out.

"It didn't seem important at the time," she told him, and brushed aside his concerns for her virginity. *She* hadn't been worried. She'd thought only to silence the ache inside her and she had. Closing her eyes, Marie started, cautiously, to rock her hips against his. "Mmmm," she said quietly, relishing the delicious sensations that movement caused, and moved again, deliberately taking him deeper.

"Oh, damn it," Davis said tightly, and dropped his head to her shoulder. Anger dissolved under the onslaught of need and pleasure.

"Could we argue about this later?" she asked,

and somehow swiveled her hips in a circular motion that nearly undid him.

She was right. No talking. Not now. Not when all he could think of was burying himself so deeply inside her, they would never be free of each other.

"Yes..." He gasped and withdrew from her only to plunge inside again. Her legs locked around his waist, she pulled him deeper with every thrust. Demanding everything he had to give and offering him all that she was.

Blind to everything but her and the overwhelmingly powerful urge to become one with her, Davis turned his back on rational thought and raced toward oblivion.

Together they hurtled along the path leading them toward a release so shattering that neither of them could have been prepared.

When they reached that pinnacle, Davis called her name and felt her arms go around him to cushion his fall.

Nine

Slowly, carefully, Davis pulled away from her and shifted to one side of Marie where he collapsed like a dead man.

Body still humming with lingering flickers of delight, Marie summoned the last of her strength and turned her head on the pillow to look at him. Love, she thought dazedly. Who would have thought it? She'd long since given up on finding love, and now that she had, she must remember that just because she loved him…it didn't mean that he loved her.

She'd gone into this with her eyes wide-open, knowing that one day Davis Garvey would get over his fascination with her and move on. That realization hadn't changed.

Still, there was nothing saying she couldn't enjoy things while they lasted.

"You okay?" he asked.

Oh, more than okay, though she didn't think she'd be confessing her undying love anytime soon.

Instead, she met his steady blue gaze and said softly, "If there's a fire or an earthquake in the next few minutes, I'm going to have to simply lay here and take it."

A half smile touched one corner of his mouth. "Me, too."

"So," she said, easing one hand off the mattress to reach out and pat his arm, "just in case, I wanted to say, *thanks.*

He blinked. "Thanks?"

Inhaling deeply, Marie realized she felt completely and utterly relaxed—from tip to toe. It was glorious. "Oh, yes. Thanks. Mmm…Davis, you were…that was…" She paused, thought for a moment, then shrugged and chuckled. "I'm at a loss for words."

He slowly pushed himself up onto one elbow and looked down at her. Strangely enough, he didn't look nearly as happy as she felt at the moment.

"Well," he said quietly, "I'm not."

Puzzled, Marie didn't have a clue why he was so grumpy. She knew darn well he'd enjoyed himself every bit as much as she had. But then, she didn't have much experience with this sort of thing. She smiled to herself at that thought. She had more experience now than she'd had an hour or two ago.

"I don't know what you've got to smile about."

Marie stared at him and grinned. "If that's true, then you underestimate yourself."

"That's not what I meant."

"What did you mean?"

"Damn it, Marie," he said tightly, "why didn't you tell me?"

"Tell you what?"

"That you were a virgin."

She snorted a laugh. "Why would I do that?"

"Because..." He shoved one hand across the top of his head in frustration. "Because you're supposed to, that's why."

"There are rules about that sort of thing?" she asked, surprised.

"Hell, yes," he snapped and sat up, clearly frustrated.

"Gee, I'm sorry," she told him, completely unapologetic. Rolling to one side, she tugged the edge of the quilt out from under her so she could yank it across her naked body. Starting to feel cold from the inside out, she suddenly wanted to cover her nudity. "I guess I forgot to study my copy of *The Beginner's Guide to Sexual Situations.*"

"Oh," he told her solemnly, "that's very funny."

"Thank you," she said, fumbling with the quilt. "We aim to please."

"Do you really?"

"You have a complaint you'd like to register?" For heaven's sake, why couldn't she get the stupid quilt off the blasted bed?

"Oh," he said, leveling her with a glance, "several."

"Perhaps it'd be better if you wrote a letter," she snapped and wondered where that gloriously indolent sensation had gone. Marie glared at him when she noticed that it was his body holding down the quilt. "Move," she said.

"Move?"

"You're on my quilt and I want it."

"Oh, pardon the hell out of me," he said, and levered himself off the mattress long enough for her to snatch the quilt up and cover herself.

"You're forgiven," she said. Then she added, "See how easy that was?"

"Damn it, Marie," he said, "this isn't a joke. You should have told me."

"Uh-huh," she said, holding the quilt up over the swell of her breasts. Raking one hand through her hair, she gave him a look that should have curled his. "And when was I supposed to do that?"

"What?" He shook his head and stared at her.

"When?" she demanded, and sat up straighter against the headboard. "Oh! I know," she went on, giving in to the rising tide of anger inside her. "When you brought your car in that first day."

"Huh?"

"Sure." Marie nodded abruptly. "When we went for that test drive, I should have said, 'Give me your keys, and by the way, did you know I'm a virgin?'"

"Marie…"

"Oh, and then later, at dinner with my family," she went on in a rush. "I could have said, 'Davis, would you please pass the lasagna to the only virgin at the table?' Of course that might have been a little embarrassing for Gina, but at least *you* would have been forewarned."

"You're being ridiculous," he said, his voice a tight, hard thread.

"Not at all," Marie went on, meeting those blue eyes of his in a staring match she was determined to win. "I'm agreeing with you. You're right, I missed several key opportunities to admit to my humble station. Just think, at the batting cages, I could have said, 'I'm a virgin, so would you mind helping Jeremy hit a home run?'"

He jumped off the bed and started pacing the room. But it was angrier than pacing really. More of a stalking. Her gaze followed him, and even though her temper was beginning to boil, she felt a different kind of burning inside as she watched him move through the darkened room.

"You should have told me tonight, damn it."

"At dinner?" She went up onto her knees, still clutching that quilt to her front like a shield. "Maybe after the waiter dumped your salad in your lap. Something along the lines of, 'Let me help you pick up that lettuce, Davis, I'm a virgin.'"

He stopped dead, swiveled his head to glare at her and Marie's breath hitched in her throat. In a shaft of moonlight, his muscular body was outlined, defined. He could have posed for a marble statue. Something titled Infuriated Lover.

Oh, wow, she had a lover.

Marie swallowed the smile that thought brought. At the moment he didn't look particularly loving, and the way this conversation was headed, their one night of lovemaking could very well be their first *and* last.

He just looked at her. "I mean you could have told me here, tonight."

"Precisely when, Davis?" she asked, crawling off the mattress to stand on her own two feet. "On the couch a while ago?" Memories rushed back at her and her knees wobbled in response. "Or here, in bed? What was the point? You found out eventually."

"Yeah, when it was too late to stop."

"Good. I didn't want you to stop."

He scraped both hands across his face, growled deep in his throat, then walked toward her. Grabbing her shoulders, he gave her a little shake and said, "Don't you get it? You deserved better your first time."

Is that what this was all about? For pity's sake. Was he grading his performance? Well, she could reassure him on that score anyway.

Lifting one hand, she cupped his cheek and looked deeply into his eyes. "I don't see how it could have been any better."

He shook his head, pulled her to him and wrapped his arms around her. Resting his chin on top of her head, he said, "That's just it. You don't see how. But I can. And if I'd known..."

If he'd known, Marie thought, he might not have gone through with it and then she would have missed out on one incredible experience. No, whatever he might think, things had worked out better this way.

She snuggled in close, letting the quilt drop between them, so that she could feel the warm brush of his flesh against hers. His heart beat steadily beneath her ear as she said, "I wouldn't change a thing, Davis. Really."

He squeezed her tight enough to snap her ribs, then eased up the pressure, still keeping her in the circle of his arms. "Why am I the one making noises about this? Damn it, Marie, you should be the one upset here."

"Why?" She tipped her head back to look up at him. "It was wonderful. I'm glad it was you. I'm glad I'm not a virgin anymore. Don't make such a big deal out of it."

"You *deserve* a big deal," he said tightly.

Didn't he have a clue just how big a deal this had been for her? Good heavens, she'd only just realized that she loved him. How many women were fortunate enough to always be able to remember their first time with the knowledge that they'd been with a man they loved?

Of course, it was very nice to have him so concerned for her feelings. But what he couldn't know was that, having realized she loved him, it made what they had shared all the more beautiful. Heck, darn near miraculous.

"I *deserve* to enjoy the lovely glow you gave me," she countered.

He laughed shortly, the sound coming harsh and strained from his throat. "Glow, huh? There are other kinds of glows, you know."

"Hmm?"

"There's something else we have to talk about," he said.

"Now what?" Really, if *she* was happy, why couldn't he be?

"We didn't use any protection, Marie."

"Protection." The first drops of rain started to land on her parade.

"I'm clean," he said quickly as if to reassure her. "And if you're on birth control pills, then we have nothing to worry about."

Birth control pills. Sure, what twenty-six-year-old virgin wasn't taking the Pill in the hopes that *someday,* someone *might* come along and *maybe* she'd finally have sex?

"Marie?"

"In a perfect world…" Okay, now she was upset. Protection. She hadn't given it a thought. Oh, brother, wouldn't it be just retribution for a virgin to get pregnant her first time out?

"No Pill?"

"No Pill."

"Oh, man." He inhaled deeply, and tightened his hold on her. "It'll be okay. It's my fault," he said. "I should have—"

"There were two of us there, Davis," she pointed out. And therein lay the problem. But she'd be darned if he'd take all the blame for this. "We're both grown-ups. We made a mistake."

"A big one."

"Well, if you're going to make a mistake," she muttered, "might as well go whole hog."

Davis stared blankly at the darkened ceiling for a long moment and mentally called himself all kinds of uncivilized names. He hadn't done anything this stupid since he was seventeen and got lucky with the girl next door.

A virgin, he thought. He'd never been with a virgin before, and the fact that Marie had allowed him to be her first both shocked and touched him. She'd trusted him to initiate her into lovemaking, and brother, had he let her down.

Not only had he taken her virginity, he might have made her pregnant. All because he hadn't been strong enough to withstand his hormones. But in his own defense, he admitted silently, it had been much more than hormones. It had felt like his very life had depended on having Marie. Being a part of her. And now, both their lives might very well change forever because of it.

Leading her to the foot of the bed, Davis sat down and dragged her onto his lap. The feel of her naked skin against his had him wanting her all over again, and that was a new sensation. Always before, once the rush of desire had been sated, he'd been content. But with Marie, being with her had only fed the hunger that continued to grow inside him. A warning bell went off in his head, but he ignored it.

"You're taking this pretty well," he said softly.

She scooted around to get comfortable, and Davis drew in a long, deep breath, hoping to keep his body from responding. It didn't help.

"Do hysterics act as an after-the-fact birth control method?" she asked with a shrug.

"Nope," he told her, and laid one hand across her thighs, trying to hold her still.

"Then what would be the point?"

Amazing woman. Over the last several days, he'd really grown to *like* Marie. Kind and patient, funny and smart, not to mention being a hell of a mechanic, Marie Santini was a frighteningly perfect woman. Now he was finding out that she was great company in a crisis situation. No losing her head. No shouting or blaming. Just a woman way too good for him. If he were a different sort of man, he might right now be thinking about getting down on his knees and begging her to marry him.

Instead, he looked into her eyes, saw the softening gleam in those green depths and had to battle down the urge to run. Marie was the kind of woman who wanted family. Hell, she *needed* family. And Davis wouldn't know what to do with a family if he fell into the middle of one.

Still, a part of him wished that he and Marie belonged together. That he could call this woman *home*.

"You're really something, you know it?" he asked, and knew it for the understatement that it was.

"Yeah," Marie said with a smile, "Jeremy says I'm the bomb."

"The bomb?"

"Apparently a good thing."

Then she was definitely the bomb.

"I want you to know," he said, "if you're pregnant—"

"I'll deal with that problem if it presents itself."

"*We'll* deal," he said firmly. He wanted her to know that in this, at least, she could trust him. He'd be there. For her. For a baby. A baby. God help them all.

She looked into his eyes and nodded. "*We'll* deal."

At least that much was settled. "When will we know for sure?"

She thought about it for a moment, then said, "Before Christmas."

Less than three weeks, he told himself. He'd lived through boot camp and combat. He could last until Christmas.

"But for now…" she said, dragging his attention back to her as she wrapped her arms around his neck.

"Yeah…?" He pulled his head back to watch her warily.

She smiled at him and he felt the power of that smile like a punch to the midsection. His body stirred and a fresh wave of need swelled inside him. Oh, he was in serious trouble when even the threat of possible parenthood wasn't enough to make him head for the door.

"We're here together.…" She tossed her hair back from her face and ran the tip of one finger along his jaw and then across his lips. "Do you have any of that protection you mentioned?"

Everything inside Davis tightened a notch or two. She'd never been with a man before tonight, a possible pregnancy was hanging in the balance and yet, here she was, rekindling the fires between them. And he was leaping into the warmth she offered.

"As a matter of fact, I do," he said, thinking of

the foil packets he'd been carrying around for the last few days in the hope he and Marie would come together. And naturally, when they did make love, he'd been so intent on her, he'd forgotten all about the little packages that could have saved them a couple weeks of worry.

She smiled at him again and it was a different smile. The age-old feminine smile that had been bringing men to their knees for centuries.

"Man," he whispered, sliding his hand up the nape of her neck to thread his fingers through the black silk of her hair, "I thought virgins were supposed to be shy...."

"But as you pointed out a few minutes ago," Marie told him as she leaned in for his kiss, "I'm not a virgin anymore."

"I stand corrected."

"Oh," she said softly, "don't stand on my account."

Two days later, Marie lay half under her mother's kitchen sink and bonked her head hard when she sat up suddenly and asked, "Was that my phone?"

"No," Gina said from her seat at the kitchen table. She turned the page of her magazine, shot Marie a quick, amused look and added, "just like it wasn't your phone ten minutes ago, too."

"So sue me," Marie snapped, and eased her head back down beneath the pipes. "I thought I heard something."

"I'm not surprised you're hearing bells the way

you slammed your head into the bottom of the sink.''

Marie ground her teeth together, gripped the wrench handle more tightly, ignored her sister and tried to turn the frozen-in-place bolt again. Damn it, she didn't have time for this. She should be at the shop working on Laura's car. She should be Christmas shopping. She should be...with Davis.

That was the real problem, here. Not her mother calling her to help out with a plugged sink. Since their night together, Marie hadn't heard a word from Davis Garvey. Nothing. No phone call, no visit to the garage, no drop-in at the apartment. It was as if in one magical night she'd found the love of her life and chased him off in the process.

"So who are we expecting to call?" Gina asked in a much-too-innocent-sounding tone. "Plumbers Unlimited?"

"Very amusing," Marie said through gritted teeth. "When is Mama going to be back from the store?"

"There's no telling. I get my love of shopping from Mom."

"Well," Marie said, "I'm never going to get this darn elbow joint off. We'll have to call a plumber."

"And tie up the phone line?" Gina countered, then *tsk-tsked*. "We wouldn't want that, would we?"

Marie squirmed out from under the sink, hefted the wrench in one hand and looked at her sister. "Watch it, Gina. I'm armed and just a little cranky."

Gina flipped the magazine closed, got up from the table and walked to where Marie was sitting on the floor. Then, squatting, she looked her sister dead in the eye. "It's Davis, isn't it?" she asked.

Marie shifted her gaze away and made a big production out of precisely placing her wrench back into the toolbox. She didn't want to get into this with Gina. She didn't want to have to admit out loud that not only had Davis left her—like every other guy she'd ever known—but that he'd left her in record time, carrying her virginity like a trophy.

Besides, she was making too big a deal out of this. She'd known all along that Davis wouldn't be interested in her forever. And yet, only two nights ago, he'd seemed very interested indeed.

"This has nothing to do with Davis," she said, forcing conviction into her voice. "It's raining, I've got work backed up at the shop and I'm hip-deep in stubborn kitchen appliances only two weeks from Christmas. Isn't that enough to make a person crabby?"

"Uh-huh," Gina said, "but not enough to make a person imagine a telephone ringing."

"A simple mistake."

"Once maybe, but twice?"

"Maybe I should try the heat gun on that bolt," Marie said. "It could warm up enough to turn."

"Who cares?"

"Mama."

"This is about Davis, isn't it?" Gina demanded. "That's why you're not looking at me. That's why you've been avoiding me for the last couple of days.''

Bingo, Marie thought, but didn't say. Gina was way too observant.

''You're nuts.''

''Then look me dead in the eye and deny you're waiting to hear from Davis.''

''Fine.'' Steeling herself to keep her emotions shuttered, Marie looked into Gina's dark brown gaze and hoped her sister wouldn't notice a thing.

''Ohmigod!'' Gina sputtered.

Marie gasped and turned away, looking back at the floor, the ceiling, the windows, the darned sink that had brought her here in the first place.

But Gina wouldn't be ignored. Not now, anyway. ''You did it, didn't you?'' she asked, plopping onto the floor and grinning. ''You and Davis did the deed!'' She whooped, clapped her hands and actually chortled, ''And the last Santini virgin bites the dust.''

Boy, her little sister was good. What did she have—radar?

Ten

Rain drummed against the canvas, convertible roof of the Mustang and pinged off its hood and fenders. Davis parked at the curb in front of the Santini house and stared through the streaming passenger side window at Marie's apartment. Was it only two days ago he'd been here? Had it really only been two days since he'd spent hours wrapped around Marie's willing, responsive body?

It felt longer.

He shoved one hand across the top of his head, then dropped that hand to the steering wheel. His fingers tapped out a rhythm to match the pounding rain as he reminded himself that he'd stayed away purposely. He'd wanted to give Marie some room. Whether she admitted it or not, what had passed between them that night *was* a big deal. And he had to be sure she'd had time to think about what she wanted to do. He'd seen that softening gleam in her eyes that night and known it for exactly what it was. Reaction to the temporary closeness of lovemaking. But she'd been a virgin. She didn't know that you could feel the same sense of intimacy with anyone.

"Liar," he muttered to himself as the inside of the windows began to fog over. He'd been with enough women to know that what he'd found in Marie's arms was unlike anything he'd ever experienced before. Something had happened between them. Something strong and elemental. Davis had touched and been touched on levels he hadn't known existed.

And then he'd stayed away.

His right hand gripped the steering wheel tightly enough to snap it in two. Hell, by now Marie might be wishing she'd never heard of Davis Garvey. And though it'd probably be better for both of them if she told him to get lost, he hoped to hell she wouldn't.

Two days without her had taught Davis one thing. How much he liked being with her. He'd missed seeing her smile, hearing her sing along to the oldies radio station she listened to. Missed the sound of her voice and her smart-aleck remarks.

Bottom line…he missed Marie.

Still, they had to talk. If they were going to keep seeing each other, then she had to know that as much as he liked her, enjoyed being with her, there was no future in this.

"Oh, good idea, Marine," he muttered darkly. Just the thing you should tell the woman who might be pregnant with your child. A flicker of something he didn't want to call fear rippled through him. A child. He shook his head. No. Wouldn't happen. No way would God sentence an innocent kid to a life with a father like him.

And on that happy thought, Davis opened the car door and stepped into the mouth of the storm.

"Give me details," Gina demanded, leaning toward her sister, an eager expression on her face.

Outside, the wind whipped rain against the windows, rattling the panes, and the winter cold seemed to seep through the glass into Marie's bones. She suddenly felt like a bug on a slide under a microscope. And knowing her sister, Marie was sure Gina wasn't going to quit until she got the information she was after.

Of course, that didn't mean she'd make it easy on Marie.

"No way," Marie snapped, shaking her head. That night was special...secret. Sharing the memory of what had happened between her and Davis would make it less real, less *hers*. And she had a feeling that as the years passed away and she lived her life alone, she'd be wanting to pull up the memories of that night. Often.

"Oh, c'mon," her younger sister prodded. "The mighty Marie finally takes the plunge—this is news."

"This is private," Marie said flatly, even though

she knew it wouldn't stop the smiling woman facing her.

The Santini family was world-renowned for their stubbornness. The two of them entered a staring contest, each of them looking for signs of weakness in the other.

A long moment passed in silence, the only sound the rain tapping wildly at the windows. Finally though, Gina's shoulders slumped in defeat. Folding her hands in her lap, she took a breath and said quietly, "At least, tell me what it was like."

An interesting development.

Marie stared at her little sister as a surprising notion presented itself. Was it possible? she wondered, tipping her head to one side to study the other woman she'd thought she'd known so well. Could it be that big-talking, always-dating Gina wasn't as experienced as she let everyone believe?

"What was it like?" Marie repeated at last. "Are you saying…?"

Gina shrugged, lifting both hands high in the air before letting them drop to her lap again. "What can I say?" she said. "I lied. You weren't the last Santini virgin. I am."

Okay, Marie thought, stunned. This little piece of news ranked right up there with finding out the world really was flat, after all. Remembering all the times she'd taken Gina's teasing about her lack of experience, Marie scowled and demanded, "Why?"

"Why not?" Gina countered, a bit defensively, Marie thought. "It's nobody's business what I do…or don't do, right?"

Amazing.

"Oh, but my business was your business?"

"Sure," Gina said with a grin. "That's what sisters are for."

Completely unrepentant and totally Gina.

"But—"

"But me no buts," Gina interrupted her. "Just tell me if I have something good to look forward to."

Good? That didn't half cover it, Marie thought, remembering the liquid heat in Davis's touch. The fires that had burned all night. The incredible sensation of reaching for a pleasure so deep, it almost scared you to claim it, only to grab it and find that it made you more complete than you ever thought you could be.

How could she explain to Gina what you couldn't possibly understand until you'd discovered it for yourself? Like tuning a carburetor, you could learn the steps, know what's expected of you, but until you rebuilt one for yourself, you just couldn't know what it was all about. And she could just imagine trying to look her sister in the eye while comparing sex to a carburetor.

Besides, how could she tell Gina how glorious it was and then admit that Davis had been avoiding her for two days? Nope, she told herself, she'd keep her comments short and sweet.

"Yeah, it's good." And as Gina smiled, Marie's eyes closed on memories and she added, "With the right person, it's wonderful."

"You're in love with him, aren't you?" Gina asked.

Marie's eyes flew open again and she stared at her sister. The brightly lit kitchen offered her no shadows to hide in, and sitting this close to the very observant Gina would make it impossible to disguise the emotion she knew was shining in her eyes. So why bother denying it?

Because that's why.

"Of course not." As a lie, it wasn't much, but it was the best she could do.

"Yeah, I'm convinced," Gina said, placing both hands on the floor behind her and leaning back.

"Good. Now leave me alone to fix this bloody sink."

"Forget the stupid sink."

"Mom thanks you."

"Marie, I know you're in love with him."

"What makes you so sure?"

"Because—you wouldn't have gone to bed with him otherwise."

Simple, but true. "*Please* leave it alone, Gina."

"Not gonna happen," she said with a slow shake of her head.

One look at Gina's determined features convinced Marie that—to borrow a quote from a popular science fiction character—"resistance was futile."

Gina sensed her sister's surrender and was prepared to be generous in victory. "So what's the problem?" she asked softly.

"How much time do you have?"

Gina grinned. "As much as you need."

"Problems, huh?" Marie asked. "Okay, let's see. I've only known him for about a minute and a half…"

"Mama and Papa only knew each other a week before they got married. Worked for them."

"That was different." Marie turned and noisily searched through the toolbox for a smaller-headed wrench. "We have nothing in common except interest in cars. And I have the distinct feeling that if anyone mentioned the word *love,* Davis would take off so fast, and so far, a marine recon platoon wouldn't be able to find him."

"Why don't you try it and find out?"

"Huh?" Marie's head snapped up and she stared at her sister as if she was nuts.

"I said, try it." Gina shrugged and smiled. "You've got nothing to lose. If he bolts, good riddance. If he doesn't, we've got another romantic Santini story to hand down the generations."

"Easy for you to say," Marie said while her mind toyed with the idea of confessing her love. But how could she set herself up for rejection like that? What was she supposed to do when after hearing her out, Davis paled and said, "Thanks but no thanks"?

No. Better to just leave secrets unsaid and enjoy whatever time she had with him.

"And here's your chance," Gina crowed, looking past Marie to the window.

Marie followed her gaze. Through the rain she saw Davis knocking on her apartment door. Her heart did a quick spin in her chest and the fingers clutching the wrench suddenly weakened, dropping the tool into the box with a clatter of sound.

He'd come back.

Before Marie could do or say anything, Gina was on her feet, racing to the back door and throwing it open. Wind-thrust rain rushed into the kitchen as she shouted, "Hey, Davis. Marie's over here."

He turned, nodded and sprinted down the steps. Coming to a stop just inside the kitchen door, he raked his gaze around the warm, bright room until he found Marie. Then he just looked at her with enough feeling that she felt her toes curl inside her shoes.

"You're right on time," Gina said, half dragging him into the room and closing the door against the storm.

Marie gave her sister a quick look. She wouldn't put it past Gina to announce, "Marie's in love with you, and what are you going to do about it?"

Apparently sensing what she was thinking, Gina grinned.

"For what?" he asked, still watching Marie.

She paused long enough to give Marie a heart attack before saying. "Mom needs that sink fixed and our little mechanic can't seem to pull it off."

Temporarily relieved, Marie shot her a glare before looking back at Davis. "You don't have to help, really. I'll get it."

Gina, standing behind Davis, waved her arms and mouthed. "Don't be dumb."

Marie ignored her.

Davis did, too.

As far as he was concerned, there was no one else in the room besides him and Marie. The minute he locked eyes with her, his chest tightened and every breath became a battle. Damn, this was going to be harder than he'd thought.

"Well," Gina said loudly enough to get their attention. "I guess I'll leave you guys to the dirty work. Here, Davis." she added, reaching for the shiny wet windbreaker he wore, "I'll hang this up on the service porch."

"Thanks," he said as he slipped out of the lightweight coat and handed it over. Gina left, and neither of them noticed. Gaze still fixed on Marie, he reminded himself that he was here to have a serious talk. To let her know that he wasn't the root-bound kind of man she needed. Unfortunately, all he could think as he stared down at the ponytailed woman in blue overalls was how much he wanted her.

To combat the sexual urges raging inside him, he went down on both knees beside her and looked under the sink. It'd be best to keep his mind busy. "What's wrong with it?"

"Just backed up," she said, leaning down for another look herself.

Davis turned his head toward her and realized her face was just a kiss away from him. His gaze dropped to her mouth, and when her teeth tugged at her bottom lip, he felt the gnawing sensation deep in his guts. Oh, man, what the hell was happening here?

"It's good to see you," she said, and he felt the brush of her breath against his cheek.

"Good to see you, too," he admitted. Good, great, fantastic. Seeing her was all of those things and more. But he wouldn't—couldn't—say so.

Instead, breaking the spell between them, he turned away, crawled beneath the sink and rolled over onto his back.

"I think the elbow joint's frozen," she said.

Amazing to think that anything could be frozen when he was on fire, but there you go. "Hand me the wrench," he said.

She did, and as he worked at the old pipes, he heard her say, "You're good with your hands. Do the marines have you doing mechanical stuff?"

"Nope," he said through gritted teeth as he forced the wrench down. "Just paperwork and riding herd on the rookies."

"A waste of talent," she said.

"Thanks," he mumbled as the joint moved beneath the pressure. The next few minutes went quickly as they worked together like a seasoned team. In no time at all, they had the pipe clear and a new elbow joint installed.

She checked out his handiwork, then smiled in approval. "Like I said, a waste of talent."

He scooted out from under the sink and took the towel Marie handed him. As he wiped the grease and dirt from his palms, he said, "I used to think about opening my own shop."

"A shop?"

"Something like Santini's, I guess," he went on, half wondering why he was telling her this. It was an old dream. One he hadn't really entertained in years. But over the last week or so, the time he'd spent at Marie's garage had somehow rekindled that nebulous dream. He'd never talked about it with anyone else, but telling Marie seemed natural. It felt *right,* sitting here in this kitchen, beside her, with the storm raging outside.

"I wanted to restore classic cars," he mused, thinking about the cars he had tucked away all over the country. He started talking and didn't stop until he'd described his dream shop and the way he would run the business. When he finally finished, Davis couldn't remember a time when he'd talked so much. Yet Marie didn't look bored, she looked interested. In him. His dreams.

"Did you do the Mustang yourself?" she asked quietly.

"Yeah," he said with a proud smile.

"Nice work."

He nodded, accepting the compliment and relishing it all the more because he knew she was well aware of what went into such a job. Most people didn't have a clue about these things. Marie and he could speak the same language.

"I also did a '56 Corvette, a '64 Thunderbird and a '69 Roadrunner," he told her.

Marie laughed and Davis realized anew how much he'd missed that sound. "What's so funny?"

"Muscle cars, every one of them," she said, still smiling. "How very male of you."

He grinned. "The relationship between a man and his car is a primal one, lady, and not to be taken lightly."

"'I stand corrected,'" she said, tossing one of his quotes back at him.

Instantly Davis did the same, saying, "'You don't have to stand on my account.'"

And in that moment, they were both thrown back into the memory of their night together. Tension rippled in the air around them. Marie held her breath, fighting down the swirling sensations fluttering to life in her stomach. The look in his eyes warmed her through, despite what she'd just heard him say. Or rather, what he *didn't* say.

In all his talk about opening a shop and restoring cars, there hadn't been a mention of family. A wife. *Her.* He clearly saw his future as a solitary one. Marie pushed the twinge of regret aside. She'd never expected him to stick around forever. In fact, she'd thought she'd seen the last of him two days ago.

She was in love with a man who, figuratively speaking, was keeping one foot outside the door, ready to run. Gazing into his eyes, she saw the desire in those blue depths and knew he found her attractive. Knew he wanted her. But she also knew it couldn't last.

On that thought, she shifted her gaze from his. "I, uh," she said, as she straightened out the toolbox, "used to think about expanding Santini's. But I don't know enough about restoration to make it work. Besides," she added, "there never seems to be enough time or money."

The back door flew open, letting another rush of rain and wind sweep in. Mama Santini groaned, slammed the door, then dropped her packages onto the kitchen table.

"Hi, Mom."

Mama gasped, clutched the base of her throat and whirled around, all in one move. "Marie! Lord, girl, you scared ten years off me. Hello, Davis. Nice to see you again."

"Ma'am..." He pushed himself to his feet, then offered a hand to Marie. She took it, and when he pulled her up, too, he kept a firm hold on her hand.

Mama noticed, but thankfully didn't say a word about it.

"The sink's fixed?" she asked.

"Yes," Marie answered, reluctantly tugging her hand free. Her fingers felt suddenly cold without the warm clasp of Davis's hand. "Davis fixed it."

"Well, thank you," Mama said with a smile. Taking off her coat and draping it cross the back of one of the chairs, she said, "You'll stay to dinner, won't you? It's only fair to let me thank you for all your hard work."

Marie slanted a look at him and was surprised to find him staring at her. His eyes held a question and she knew he was waiting to see if *she* wanted him to stick around. She met his gaze squarely and echoed her mother's request, though she was hoping for much more than just dinner.

"Please stay."

He nodded, then glanced at her mother. "Thank you, ma'am, I believe I would like to stay for a while."

A while, he'd said, and Marie had a feeling he,

too, was referring to more than just dinner. He wanted to stay…be with her, for *a while.* She wondered just how long he considered a while to be and knew that even if he'd meant years, it wouldn't be long enough for her.

The next few hours passed quickly. Though he and Marie were surrounded by family every minute, he'd discovered that he didn't feel nearly as out of place as he had before. And Davis wasn't sure if that was a good thing or a bad thing. Becoming used to the feeling of being sucked down by quicksand didn't prevent a person from sinking. It only served to blind you to the coming danger.

Davis helped Angela set up her new CD player, wiring in the speakers and laughing with the family when Jeremy insisted on playing his CD first. They all stoically sat through what seemed like years' worth of children's folk songs, though he managed to avoid joining in on the choruses. While the women went in to finish dinner and set the table, he and Jeremy played video games.

"This is cool that you're here," the boy said, and pushed a button that destroyed Davis's onscreen car.

He winced and pushed his own button, but nothing happened. What is it with kids? he wondered. Were they born knowing how to play these things?

"My dad died, y'know." Jeremy said suddenly, and Davis looked at him.

"Yeah, I know." A pang of sadness for the boy rose up inside him. Davis knew all too well what it was to lose a parent. But at least Jeremy still had his mother and grandmother and two aunts who loved him. The kid was luckier than a lot of others his age.

Luckier than Davis had been.

"I don't really remember him," Jeremy was saying.

Davis thought that was probably best. If he did remember, he'd only torture himself with memories and spend his free time constructing imagined "what if" scenarios. As he himself had done for too long.

"And except for me, it's always all girls around here," Jeremy said with a sneer, "so I like it when you come over."

"Thanks," Davis said, smiling. The boy was learning early to take comfort from his own kind. "I like it, too." In fact, it surprised him how much he was enjoying himself.

The house was cozy and filled with a warmth that seemed to beckon a person farther inside. Laughter and hushed conversation flowed from the kitchen, and Davis caught himself listening for the sound of Marie's voice.

"Why don't you marry Marie and then you can be here all the time?" Jeremy said.

Swiveling his head to look at the boy, Davis just stared at him for a long minute or two, wondering what to say.

"I mean," the kid continued, sparing Davis a reply, "I'd like it if my mom got married again even better. 'Cause having a father would be pretty awesome. But havin' an uncle would be pretty good, too.''

Uncle. Uncle Davis.

Damn. He was fairly sure he liked the sound of that. Frowning to himself, Davis felt the unmistakable suction of quicksand pulling him under.

Jeremy set his game paddle down on the floor in front of him and turned to look at him. When he didn't get the man's attention, he patted his knee until Davis looked at him.

"Can you come back tomorrow evening?'' he asked quietly, shooting a nervous look toward the kitchen, as if hoping the females would keep themselves scarce.

"Why tomorrow?'' Davis asked.

Jeremy leaned into him and whispered in a voice that could have been heard in Chicago, "Because tomorrow we go to get our Christmas tree, and if you don't come then we can't go to the chop-it-down place.''

"Why not?''

"'Cause a girl can't chop down a tree." Disgusted, Jeremy shook his head.

"Is that right?'' Davis asked, smiling at the boy's scowl.

"Everybody knows that. That's how come we always go to the grocery store to buy one.''

"Ah…''

"So will ya?''

Christmas tree shopping. "Uncle Davis." He was getting in too deep here, and for the life of him, couldn't find a way out. Looking into the boy's eager expression, he knew that way out didn't lead across Jeremy's wounded feelings. So, he thought, Christmas tree shopping it was. After all, there was a first time for everything. And it was a good excuse to see Marie again. "Sure."

"Promise?" the boy asked, studying his face.

He thought about it for a moment, knowing that once he'd given his word, he wouldn't break it. Did he really want to do this? And a voice inside him whispered, *"Yes."*

"Promise."

Eleven

The evening with the Santini family was over, and Marie led Davis up the steps to her apartment. For the last few hours, she'd watched him with her family. Had seen how easily he fit in and how much her mother, sisters and nephew liked him. And yet she hadn't been blind to the fact that even while enjoying himself, Davis had held a part of himself back.

Only a couple of weeks ago, she hadn't known Davis Garvey existed. She'd lived her life and thought it complete. She'd been *happy,* if a little lonely. But now that he'd entered her life, she knew that once he left it, happiness would never be harder to find.

The rain had slackened off to a drizzle that dampened her clothes and seemed to soak right down to her bones. A chill crept over her, but Marie had the strangest sense that it had nothing to do with the weather. In her heart she was already preparing for him to leave.

As she sensed he was.

The door swung wide and the single lamp she'd left burning cast a soft, golden light over the small living room. Her gaze went directly to the over-stuffed sofa where Davis had first made love to her and she knew she'd never be able to enter this room without remembering every tiny detail of that night.

Even thinking about it made her body burn and hum with a kind of frenzied energy. And knowing that whatever she had with Davis wasn't permanent did nothing to smother the flames she felt inside.

She closed the door behind him, and when she turned around, he was there. Just inches from her. She tipped her head back to look up at him, and her breath caught at the expression on his face. Desire, tenderness, regret, all pooled together and simmered in his eyes. A deeply throbbing ache settled around her heart.

"Marie…" He reached for her, and she caught his hand in hers, curling her fingers around his. "We have to talk. About the other night. About what's between us."

Was it just her, or was the word *goodbye* hidden in that statement? Marie didn't want to hear it. Not tonight. Not now. She wanted one more night with him. Well, actually, she wanted a lifetime's worth of nights with Davis. But she would settle for one more…before he turned and stepped out of her life.

She held on to his hand and brought it up to her face. Then, nuzzling her cheek against his palm, she said, "Don't talk, Davis. Not now."

He pulled in a long, shuddering breath and she watched different emotions chase each other across his features. But finally, regret was eased aside to be replaced by desire, and Marie knew that this one time, at least, she'd won.

"This is a mistake," he said quietly, even as he moved in closer to her. "We're too different. We want different things."

"Tonight," she said just as softly, "we want the same thing. Each other."

"Yeah," he muttered, "you're right about that," and cupped her face in his palms, tipping her mouth up to meet his. The kiss began as a gentle brush of lips against lips, but the instant their mouths met, an urgency burst into life between them.

He devoured her, his tongue opening her lips for his invasion, and when he swept inside her warmth, Marie leaned into him, groaning her surrender. Again and again he stroked her tongue with his, electrifying her bloodstream and sending shivers of expectation from the roots of her hair to the tips of her toes.

Marie wrapped her arms around his neck and held on, feeling as though she was sitting in the lead car on a roller coaster. Highs and lows seemed more frantic, more pulse pounding. Her stomach pitched, her mouth went dry and even the palms of her hands itched for him.

Hunger, raw and powerful roared through her,

leaving her shaken but determined. She pulled at his windbreaker and he let her go long enough to tear it and his shirt off, baring his chest for her exploring hands. Then he turned his nimble fingers to the brass catches of her overalls. He flicked them open, and the overalls dropped to below her waist. Then he grabbed the hem of her tiny tank top and yanked it up and over her head.

The rush of cool air against her bare breasts puckered her nipples and Marie groaned again, more loudly this time, when Davis dipped his head to take first one, then the other into his mouth. Sensations rose up and shattered inside her. Incredible, the swell of emotions churning within. She clutched at his shoulders and his arms came around her, lifting her, bracing her back against the closed front door. The shock of the cold wood along her spine made her gasp and that gasp only built as she felt him ease her overalls and then her panties down and off her legs.

Free of her clothes, Marie gave herself up to the wildness rattling around within and wrapped both legs around his waist. He dipped his head, kissing her nipples one after the other. Tasting, sucking, nipping at their sensitive tips, he pushed her higher, higher, closer to the edge of the precipice she knew was waiting for her. She leaned her head back against the door and stared unseeing at the ceiling while Davis did unimaginable things to her body…to her soul.

One strong arm supported her while Davis's other hand dropped. She heard the unmistakable sound of a zipper being yanked down and everything within her tightened. Soon, she told herself. Soon, she'd feel him inside her again. Know that sense of completion again.

"Damn it," he muttered thickly, and Marie forced herself out of the sexual fog settling over her brain.

Breathless, she asked, "What? What is it?"

"I can't do this one-handed," he said, and every word sounded as though it had been squeezed from his throat.

She opened her eyes, looked at the small foil packet he held and understood. "Let me," she said, and reached for it.

He gave it to her and kept his gaze locked with hers as she ripped the foil and pulled the condom from its wrappings. Letting her slide down against the door, Davis held her steadily as she reached for him. Slowly, tenderly, she smoothed the satin-thin material down over the length of him and he winced with the effort to hold himself in check.

"Marie…" He said her name on a moan, and the sound of his need fed her own.

She couldn't wait. Couldn't stand the tension coiling inside her. She needed him with a desperation she never would have thought possible. Marie closed her eyes and bit down hard on her bottom lip before saying softly, "Now, Davis. Please, now."

"Now," he echoed, and still bracing her against the door, slid himself home.

She gasped and arched into him, instinctively drawing him deeper inside. He buried his face in the curve of her neck and groaned like a dying man granted a last-minute pardon.

After savoring their joining for a brief moment, Davis withdrew from her only to plunge back inside deeper, harder. Her legs held him to her, her hands clawed at his back as she felt the tightness inside her grow and build. Higher, faster than ever before, they raced together toward the edge of oblivion, and when they found it, they tumbled into the abyss together, safe in each other's arms.

Before the last tremor shuddered through her body, Marie whispered, "I love you." And in the very next instant she knew she'd said the wrong thing.

Davis went utterly and completely still.

The echo of those three little words burrowed inside him and wrapped themselves around his heart. He closed his eyes against the warmth suddenly spreading through him. He couldn't remember ever hearing those words directed at him before. And now that they had been, he didn't know what to say. Or do.

Slowly, carefully, he disengaged himself from her and gently set her back on her feet. In these first awkward moments, a strained silence slammed down between them and he was grateful she didn't say anything more.

This was his own fault. He'd let himself get too close. Let *her* get too close. And now there was no way to leave her without hurting her.

"Davis," she said, and he knew the temporary silence was finished. Now he'd have to talk and say the things he knew would tear at her heart and soul. He had to refuse the gift she'd offered him. Have to tell her that there was no future for her with a man who had no past.

"Marie," he said quickly, wanting to stop her before she said those words again. "I'm not looking for anything permanent."

"I didn't say you were," she said.

His gaze snapped to her. "But you said—"

She actually smiled at him. It was sad, regretful, but still a smile. "I said I love you. I do."

He flinched. He'd never expected to hear those words. Had never put himself in the position where he *might* hear them. Hell, he didn't know squat about love. About loving. Now, if she wanted to know how to pull together a recon mission in less than twenty-four hours, he was her man. He could field-strip a machine gun and have it back together again in less time than it took to think about it. He could do a hundred push-ups without breaking a sweat, and if the corps demanded it, he could find a way to walk on water.

But damn it, when it came to love, *she* was the expert and he was as blind and stupid as any first-week grunt in boot camp.

"You and I, what we have together is...*good*," he finished with feeling, even knowing that "good" was a major understatement. What he'd found with her was more than he'd ever thought existed.

"It's more than good," she said, as if reading his thoughts, "but I think you know that."

His back teeth ground together and every cell in

his body stiffened. Why was she being so damned *nice?* Any other woman would be dragging him over hot coals about now. But then, no other woman before Marie had ever claimed to love him. Of course she'd react differently than he'd expect. "Don't make this harder on both of us," he said.

"Don't worry," she said, and hooked the last of the buckles on her overalls.

He just stared at her. She hadn't bothered to put her top back on, so the overalls barely covered her breasts. Her black hair was mussed, her eyes were overly bright and her mouth swollen from his kisses. And Davis wanted her more than life itself.

Which is what had gotten him into this mess in the first place. Curling his hands into helpless fists at his sides, he waited for her to go on. Waited to give her the time to work up to telling him off. As he deserved.

"I didn't mean to say the words out loud," she continued. "It just sort of…slipped out."

She was *apologizing* to him? "Damn it, Marie," he said tightly, "*yell* at me. Throw something. Jeez, at least tell me what a bastard I am!"

She shook her head and chuckled humorlessly. "It wouldn't help."

It'd sure as hell help him, he wanted to say. It would relieve some of the overwhelming guilt that had settled in the pit of his stomach, making him feel cold all over. But then, he didn't have the right to feel better, did he? This wasn't about him. It was about her.

"Marie," he said, "I don't want to hurt you."

"I know that."

"Don't expect more from me than I can give."

"I don't expect anything from you, Davis." She said it sadly, with a slow shake of her head.

"You should," he said.

"Why? So I can be disappointed?" She shook her head again and walked past him to the sofa. There she sat down and curled her feet up under her. "No, thanks. But I won't make this any easier on you, either, Davis. I can't pretend I don't love you. I do."

Davis winced inwardly and fought his instinct to run. Hell. What kind of marine was he that three little words could make him turn tail like this? And what kind of man was he that he could face down armed-to-the-teeth enemies but a woman declaring her love brought him to his knees?

"I understand you don't love me back," she said quietly. "I guess it just happens that way sometimes," she added, her voice getting smaller, quieter. "Fate playing little jokes."

"Marie…"

"It's okay, Davis," she said, and folded her arms across her chest. "It really is. Some people you love. Some you don't."

It wasn't okay. Nothing about this was okay.

"Marie, I care for you," he said, and knew it wasn't enough. Would never be enough for her.

A tiny, almost-not-there smile touched her mouth briefly. "I'm sure you do, Davis. But caring isn't loving, is it?"

"No." He squeezed that word past the knot in his throat and watched it hit her like a bullet. A prize bastard, that's what he was. But even knowing that didn't change a damn thing.

"Davis...if you don't mind, I'm kind of tired, so..."

She wanted him to leave.

Not so surprising, he told himself. Why wouldn't she? She confesses her love and he shuts down like an unplugged computer. Emptiness welled up inside him, and it felt as though a black hole had opened wide to swallow his heart and the barren thing most people would call his soul.

He should have been better prepared for tonight. He'd known all along his time with Marie would end. Davis didn't have relationships. He had encounters. Brief, fiery, encounters. This was the first time he'd actually gotten to know a woman. Like her. And though it was illogical and irrational, he couldn't help feeling disappointed that she hadn't even *asked* him to stay. It didn't make any sense at all, but he wanted her to want him to stay even if he couldn't.

No one had *ever* asked him not to leave.

And in this, at least, Marie was no different from the rest.

"All right," he said quietly. "I'll go." Then, remembering, he added, "But until we know for sure about whether or not there's a baby, I won't go far."

"Oh, Davis," she said, and her voice was barely above a whisper. "You're already so far away, I can't reach you."

She was right. And he could only hope that a benevolent God would have the good sense to *not* sentence an innocent baby to a life with him as its father.

He inhaled sharply, took one last look at her, opened the door and stepped outside. It didn't surprise him at all when the skies burst like a popped water balloon and drenched him with a wall of rain.

He deserved nothing less.

A cold wind raced through the tiny forest of perfectly sculpted pine trees. The fresh clean scent of the Christmas tree lot filled the air, and the thick layer of sawdust covering the bare earth behind their feet muffled their footsteps. Dozens of people wandered up and down the aisles, admiring, then dismissing the pines in the quest for the perfect Christmas tree.

From a small wooden snack stand near the office came the aromas of hot chocolate, hot dogs and popcorn. The sky overhead was cloudy, but the sun continued to peek in and out, giving the lot a dappled, shady look that only fed into the feeling that Christmas was just around the corner.

And in the midst of happy families and professional carolers, two people stood uneasily, staring at each other.

"You didn't have to do this," Marie said for the third time in five minutes.

Davis looked down at her, shoved his hands into his jeans pockets and nodded. "Yes, I did," he said. "I promised."

He'd promised. That's what he'd said when he'd turned up at the Santini house a half an hour ago.

Marie hadn't actually expected him to show up. Not after what had happened the night before. But apparently, she'd underestimated Sergeant Davis Garvey's sense of duty.

At least Jeremy was happy, she thought, her eyes skimming the crowds for her nephew. But the boy had disappeared again. He'd spent the last fifteen minutes darting in and out of the trees like a young Daniel Boone. In fact, he was having the time of his life, completely unaware of any discomfort between the adults accompanying him.

"Look, Marie," Davis said, and something inside her cringed. She didn't want to talk about last night again. She didn't want to remember, as she had all during the sleepless hours of the longest night of her life, the look on his face when she'd blurted, "I love you."

"Jeremy's having a good time," she said in an effort to keep their conversation centered on the hunt for a Christmas tree. Darn it. Why hadn't Gina or Angela come along for the ride? Why had they left her alone with the man who was breaking her heart by inches?

"Yeah, he is," Davis said, never taking his gaze from her.

Tugging the cowl-necked collar of her sky-blue sweater a bit higher, Marie said only, "He would have understood though, if you hadn't shown up. I could have explained."

He snorted a choked laugh. "Explain what? That a marine was too scared to face his aunt, so instead he broke his word to a kid?"

"I could have come up with something," she insisted. And it would have been far easier than this. A dull, throbbing ache started up around her heart and it seemed as though it grew with every pulse beat. How hard it was to stand so close and yet so far from him. To remember the feel of his arms around her and the soft brush of his breath on her flesh and to know that she'd never experience that again.

"No reason for you to," Davis argued, dragging her attention away from her lovely self-pity party. "Kids have a right to expect an adult to keep his word."

Something flickered in his blue eyes, and she thought she caught a flash of remembered pain in his expression. It's not just Jeremy he's talking about, she told herself, and wondered what broken promises Davis had weathered as a boy. And if they'd had anything to do with shaping the man he was now.

"There he is," Davis said suddenly, and pointed off down the aisle on the right.

"Guess we'd better catch up to him." Marie started walking and tried not to enjoy it too much when Davis fell into step beside her.

"This is nice," he said, glancing around him at the lot and the strings of colored lights hanging overhead.

"Yes," she said, willing to talk about anything other than last night. How difficult could it be? They'd spend an hour together and then he'd be gone, leaving her to lick her wounds in private.

"We've never been here before, though Jeremy's always wanted to."

"Grocery store lots," he said.

She laughed quietly. "He told you."

"Of course."

Marie searched for something else to say and finally came up with "Actually, to me, these are not really Christmas trees."

"Could have fooled me," he said, shrugging his shoulders.

Was it her imagination or did his shoulders look even broader in that plain black sweatshirt? Immediately she pushed that thought aside and grasped at the dangling thread of conversation.

"Nope," she went on firmly. "A nice Douglas fir. That's my kind of tree. It's tradition. What we've always had."

He nodded vaguely.

"What about you?" she asked, determined to have a nice, civilized conversation, even if she had to drag words from him. If she was dying inside, she didn't have to let him know it. "What kind of tree did your family go in for?"

He reached out a hand and dragged it through the long needled boughs of the trees they passed. "Plastic."

"Fake trees?" she asked, and couldn't hide the dismay in her voice. "Oh, no."

"Oh, yeah." Davis shook his head and stuffed his hand back into his pocket. "One place I remember had a pink plastic tree and they had a colored light wheel they used to shine on it every night. Looked hideous.''

One place? she thought.

''And then another time, there was no tree at all. But I remember thinking the menorah was kind of pretty.''

Menorahs and pink trees?

''Where did you grow up, Davis?'' she asked.

''St. Louis,'' he answered stiffly, then slowly turned his head until he was looking at her. ''In a series of foster homes.''

How sad, she thought, and instantly ached for the child he'd been. ''What about your parents?''

He shrugged as if trying to rid himself of a years-old burden. ''My mother died when I was about Jeremy's age.''

She couldn't imagine anything worse than not being able to grow up as she had, safe in the knowledge of her parents' love. ''I'm so sorry, Davis.''

''Long time ago.'' He inhaled sharply, deeply.

''What about your father?''

''My father put me up for adoption a few months later.''

He sounded so cold, so matter of fact, his voice, as much as what he'd said, tore at her. What a horrible way to grow up. Never knowing a place to call your own. Never having a family to depend on. *Knowing* that your only living parent gave you away.

Maybe, she thought, this was part of the reason behind Davis's wariness about love. Maybe being denied something for most of your life left you unable to accept it when it was finally offered.

"Davis, I don't know what to say."

"Nothin' to say," he told her. He pulled one hand free of his pocket and shoved it along the side of his head. Mind spinning, Davis wondered why in the hell he'd chosen to tell her the story of his childhood. He never talked about the past. Tried not to think about it.

"It must have been awful for you," she said softly.

He stiffened at the sympathy in her tone. He didn't want pity. Didn't need it. A big woman pushing a screaming kid in a stroller passed them and Davis waited until she was a few steps farther away before saying, "Don't feel sorry for me, Marie. I don't need your sympathy."

"Don't you?" she asked, and her green eyes became warm and liquid.

He steeled himself against that soft expression of hers and reminded both of them, "It was a long time ago. I'm not that lonely kid anymore."

"I think you're wrong, Davis," she said, and reached out to lay one hand on his forearm. Even through the thick fabric of his sweatshirt, he felt a trickle of her warmth seep into his bones, swirl into his bloodstream.

And for one brief, incredible moment, he felt alive again. As alive as he felt every time he joined his body to hers. Then she spoke again and the moment was gone.

"I think there's still some of that boy in you,

Davis.'' She looked up at him, silently daring him to look away. He didn't. ''A boy who didn't have a family, so he told himself he didn't need one. A boy without love who convinced himself love wasn't necessary.''

Every word she uttered chipped away at the hard, protective shell he'd erected around his heart so many years ago. Every glance, every touch, warmed a soul that had been cold ever since he could remember.

And still he fought her.

If he admitted, even to himself, just how much Marie and even her family had come to mean to him, then he'd have to acknowledge just how much he'd missed in his life. And how much he would go on missing because he couldn't bring himself to tear down the wall he'd built up around himself.

''I can't change what happened to you when you were a child, Davis,'' she said. ''And only you can change the way you live your life now.''

Could he? he wondered. Or was it far too late for him to be anything more than he already was? Could a man who knew nothing about love really learn to give and accept it? A part of him wanted badly to believe it was possible.

''Hey, you guys!'' Jeremy shouted at them, and his voice arrived a split second before he slid to a stop beside Davis, kicking sawdust up into the air.

''What's up, kiddo?'' Marie asked, giving the boy a forced, too-hearty smile.

''I found it,'' he said with a grin. ''The perfect tree.'' He grabbed Marie's hand and started pulling her after him. "C'mon, before somebody else gets it!"

She threw an over-the-shoulder glance at Davis, and the emotions churning in her eyes nearly staggered him. She loved him. Marie Santini actually loved him. Now the question was, was he man enough to do something about that?

Grumbling to himself, Davis followed after Jeremy and Marie. He was grateful the kid had found the tree he wanted, because at the moment there was nothing Davis would like more than to chop at something with an ax.

Twelve

"**A**ll I'm saying is that you could at least *fight* for him."

Marie glared at her younger sister. Between college break and only working part-time, Gina was around far too much lately. Gina had been saying the same blasted thing for three days now, and it was getting old. As if Marie didn't want to fight for him. As if she didn't want to have him here, with her. But damn it, she had *some* pride, didn't she?

She'd told Davis she loved him. She'd told him it was up to him to decide how he wanted to spend the rest of his life...with her or alone. What more could she do?

Gina answered that question for her.

"You ought to go down to that base, look Davis dead in the eye and tell him you love him."

She choked out a strained laugh. "Gee, what a keen idea. Too bad it won't work."

"How do you know unless you try?"

"What makes you think I didn't?"

Gina sat down hard on a stool by the workbench. "You're kidding. You told him you love him and he left anyway?"

"Amazing, huh?" Marie retorted, then bent over the engine of Laura's Honda again. The darn thing was back in the shop. Her mind wasn't on work. It was, as it had been, on Davis. Still, a part of her realized that she'd have to find a cheap used car for her friend. No way was this poor Honda going to keep running for another year.

"Jeez, honey, I'm sorry."

Marie winced beneath Gina's sympathy and understood just what Davis had meant when he'd told her he didn't want her pity.

"Why didn't you tell me to shut up or something?"

Marie straightened briefly, pinned the other woman with a look and reminded her, "I have been telling you that for three days."

Gina shrugged and gave her an "oops" look. "So I don't listen as well as I talk."

"Now there's a news flash."

"Hey, I'm on your side, remember?"

"How can I forget?" Marie asked, turning her attention back to the dirty spark plugs. "You, Angela and Mama keep reminding me of that while you're all telling me how to fix my life."

"Well, somebody has to," Gina snapped.

One eyebrow lifted. "Like your life is so perfect."

Gina jumped off the stool, marched across the concrete floor, leaned both hands on the Honda's fender, looked at her sister and said, "Look, if you don't want my help, just say so. There's no reason to be insulting."

"Good." Marie glanced at her. "I don't want your help."

"Man," Gina huffed, "who would have thought a man could make you so crabby? I thought sex was supposed to improve your outlook, not ruin it." Stepping back and away from the car, she turned for the set of open double doors. "Since I'm not needed, I'll just go home."

"Good plan." Finally. Peace.

But the minute Gina left, the silence in Santini's crowded in on Marie. A twinge of guilt poked at her. She shouldn't have come down so hard on her sister. It wasn't as if it were Gina's fault Marie was so miserable.

Sighing, she straightened up again, gave the Honda's tire a good kick and resigned herself to the fact that she wouldn't be getting any work done today, either. The garage seemed too empty. Her own breath practically echoed in the quiet. She'd thought she wanted to be alone. But now that she was, alone didn't sound so great.

She tossed the wrench she held on to the rolling mechanic's bench and walked to the doorway. Gray skies and a sullen, cold wind did nothing for her mood. Stuffing her hands into the pockets of her overalls, she tried not to remember the last time she'd worn them. She fought to keep at a distance the memory of her overalls dropping to her living room floor. She didn't want to recall the feel of the cold door pressing against her back as Davis took her wildly, passionately to a world she'd never hoped to enter.

But despite her best efforts, the memories came, flooding into her mind, one after the other, never pausing, never giving her a chance to catch her breath. His eyes, his hands, his mouth, his voice. All these things and more she remembered in vivid detail and wondered hopelessly how long the memories could last. What? Twenty, thirty years, tops?

"Oh, man..."

"Marie?"

She jumped, startled and half turned to look at her mother. Maryann Santini stood watching her, a worried expression stamped on her familiar features.

"Mama?" Marie said past a sudden, tight knot lodged in her throat. "What are you doing here?"

The older woman shook her graying head. "What? I can't stop by to say hello?"

"Sure, it's just—" Understanding shone in Mama's eyes and Marie felt her resolution to be strong, crumbling. The tears she'd been holding at bay for three long days and even longer nights quickly pooled in her eyes, blurring her vision. She gulped hard and gave into the misery aching inside. "Mama...why doesn't he love me?"

Mama held her arms out and Marie stepped into them, just as she had when she was a child. And just like then, she felt the strong net of Mama's love surround her.

"What do you mean you don't have the reports finished yet?" Davis practically snarled into the telephone. The corporal on the other end of the line stammered some half-witted excuse and Davis cut him off. "Save the stories and get the damn work done by this afternoon. Understood?"

He dropped the receiver into its cradle and stared at the black phone as if it was behind all of his problems. Hell, he knew he was overreacting. A month ago, he wouldn't have cared if the corporal was a little late.

Now, though, it seemed the smallest things could set him off. He'd noticed that his fellow marines were walking a wide berth around him, and he couldn't blame them. Hell, if he could have figured a way to do it, *he* wouldn't spend any time with him, either.

The last three days without Marie had been the longest of his life. His apartment seemed lonelier, his world emptier and his future...too damned depressing to think about.

Marie. It all came back to Marie. He'd walked away, leaving everything unresolved between them. For some idiotic reason, he'd convinced himself that he *could* walk away, as he had done so many times before. But it had been impossible. Not seeing her didn't help any; his mind just conjured up memories of her face, her hands, her voice, her laugh.

He'd told her that he wouldn't go far until they

knew if they'd made a baby or not. But what would he use for an excuse to stay close once that information was in? And what if there *was* a baby?

At that thought, a tiny flicker of light flashed for an instant, deep within him. Was it *hope?*

Jumping up from his chair, he paced the office. Back and forth he went, his combat boots smacking into the worn linoleum floor with an even regularity that pounded in his head like a second heartbeat. On his third time around the room, he paused briefly at a small window and stared down at the base stretching out below him.

Marines, going about their business, hustled across the tarmac. From a distance, he heard the muted roar of the helicopters as the chopper pilots flew training exercises. Trucks loaded with supplies rolled past his building and everything looked as it should.

For more years than he wanted to remember, this base and others like it had been his world. It had always been enough, too. The corps had given him what he'd been cheated out of as a boy. Family. A place to belong. A sense of pride and accomplishment. Honor and duty.

It was who he was, he told himself as he stared down at the faceless marines going about their work. This place, this life was all he had. All he'd ever had.

Turning around slowly, he stared at his desk across the room and his gaze landed on a certain sheaf of papers. His reenlistment was due. If he didn't re-up, he'd be out of the corps within six months.

He caught himself at the thought. *"If?"* he said softly. He always signed the papers. Never considered *not* signing them.

Until now.

Suddenly his future opened up in front of him. Davis saw himself moving from one base to the next, always packing and unpacking in strange apartments. Always alone. Always starting over. Never belonging. Never having ties to anyone or anything beyond his stretch in the corps.

And when he faced mandatory retirement, he wondered, what then? Who would he be? What would he have to show for his life? A string of commendations? A few more ribbons on a uniform he could no longer wear?

Davis reached up and laid one hand against the window jamb. His vision blurred as he stared past today and into the years ahead. He would be alone, as he always had been. He would have lived his life on the edges of real life. He would have spent years, closed up on himself. Not touching or being touched. Not loving or being loved.

His fingers curled tight around the wooden molding and his back teeth ground together.

For the first time, he realized that the years ahead looked as empty as those behind him. An instant later, in a blinding flash of insight, Davis acknowledged that sort of future didn't fit him anymore. He'd tasted belonging. He'd seen what being loved could be like. And he couldn't go back to being the

way he was. A future without Marie in it was just
too bleak to consider.

The image of her face swam to the surface of his
mind and he started thinking again, as he had for
the last three days, about everything she'd said to
him that day at the Christmas tree lot. Started thinking about a lot of things.

When he was a kid, he could remember lying in
the dark, wishing things were different. Wishing he
had a place to call home. Now he was finally being
given a chance at that gift and he, like an idiot, was
running from it. Afraid he'd be found lacking somehow. Afraid he'd mess it up and have nothing.

"A helluva thing," he muttered grimly as he
slammed a fist into the wall. "A *marine* running
scared."

"You having a nightmare?" a deep voice startled
him and Davis looked up as Gunner Sergeant Nick
Peretti strolled into their shared office.

"Nightmare?"

"Yeah," Nick said on a laugh. "A marine,
scared?"

Davis laughed, too, but there was no humor in it.

Nick noticed. Sympathetically he said, "It's a
woman, isn't it?"

"Not just any woman," Davis told him. "*My*
woman. If I haven't blown it all to hell."

The other man's eyebrows went straight up. "Is
there something you'd like to share with the class?"

Davis laughed aloud, crossed the room and
slapped Nick on the back heartily enough to stagger
him. "Not just yet, Teacher. I'll let you know."

As he headed for the door, Nick shouted, "Good luck!"

"I'll need it," he called back, and hoped to God he hadn't come to his senses too late.

"All right now. Dry your eyes," Mama said sternly, handing Marie a tissue.

She did as she was told, and when she was through, she shook her head. "I don't know what to do, Mama. I mean, I knew he'd leave eventually. I just didn't expect it to hurt this badly."

Mama caught her daughter's chin in her hand and turned her face up. "What do you mean, you knew he'd leave?"

"Every other guy I've ever liked has."

"And you think you know why?"

"Sure," Marie told her. "I'm not pretty and perky like Gina or Angela. I'm a mechanic, for Pete's sake."

"So what's wrong with that?" Mama's voice took on a fighting edge.

"Nothing," Marie said quickly. "I like what I do. It's just not very…girlie."

"And do you think Davis liked Gina or Angela better than you?"

"No," she said with a half smile, remembering how tense Davis got while waiting for Gina to be quiet for a while.

"So, he doesn't mind you're a mechanic?"

"No." she said, thinking about it as she said it. "But that's not the only problem, Mama. He's never had a family. He doesn't think he knows how to belong. How to love.''

''Piffle.''

''What?'' Marie laughed and looked at her mother.

''So he's never had a family. So what? He was never in the marines until he joined, was he?'' Mama patted Marie's cheek and leaned in to say, ''A person can learn, Marie, honey. With enough love, anything is possible.''

That was the problem though, wasn't it? He didn't love her. Or if he did, he didn't love her enough.

''It's up to you, what you want to do,'' Mama said as she stood up and smoothed out the fall of her dress. ''But if it was me, I wouldn't be so quick to give up.''

''I don't know....'' She wanted to think there was a chance, but wouldn't that just be keeping her hopes up for another crash landing?

''You think about it,'' Mama said. ''Maybe,'' she added, ''if you expect him to stay, he will. Meanwhile, I'm going home to get Jeremy ready for his Christmas pageant. You coming home to change?''

''No. I brought my things here. I'll just meet you guys at the school.''

''Okay. Don't be late, though. Those kids're so excited, the play is bound to be entertaining.''

She waved and walked off down the sidewalk toward home. It was a long walk, but Mama insisted she liked the exercise. Marie watched her go, her mind racing with thoughts, hopes, dreams.

Two hours later, Marie looked into the bathroom mirror and fluffed her hair one last time. She gave herself a quick once-over and decided she looked pretty good, considering she'd been crying her eyes out only a couple of hours ago.

There was a new determination in her eyes and a firm set to her chin, too. She'd thought about what Mama said and had made up her mind to go see Davis in the morning. She'd face him down on his own turf and *order* him to admit to loving her. No way was she going to give up on him—*them*—this easily.

If he thought the marines were a tough outfit, he just hadn't seen the Santinis in high gear.

Grinning at her reflection, Marie put her holly wreath earrings on, affixed the holly pin Jeremy had made for her to the left shoulder of her lemon-yellow sweater, then left. She'd already locked the service bay doors, so she walked through the office and out the door, locking it behind her.

It wasn't until she turned around that she saw him.

Standing alongside the Mustang parked in her driveway, Davis, in full uniform, stood watching her. It was the first time she'd ever seen him in his marine uniform and she had to admit, he made quite a picture. Tall, muscular and so handsome, he took her breath away, he looked like a recruiting poster for the corps.

And she was reading a lot of hope into his coming to see her.

She walked down the driveway and stopped a few

feet from him. "Hi," she said, "I didn't expect to see you here."

"I know." He nodded abruptly, then turned toward his car. "I have something for you."

Confused, Marie watched as he dragged a live Christmas tree—a two-foot pine in a terra-cotta pot—from the back seat of the Mustang. A huge red bow was attached to its tip and the ends of the ribbon fluttered wildly in the breeze. Davis staggered under the potted tree's weight as he carried it up the driveway. He set it down in front of her and Marie looked from the pine to him.

"What's this about?" She fought to slow down the rapid beat of her heart, but lost the battle. Just being close to him was enough to send her system into overdrive, and she'd just have to accept it.

He braced his feet wide apart, folded his arms across his broad chest and said simply, "It's a Scotch pine."

"I can see that," she said with a small smile. "Why is it here?"

A slightly disgusted look crossed his face briefly as he admitted. "It's here because I couldn't find a Douglas fir." He shook his head in frustration. "Went to three nurseries before I settled for this one."

He had gone looking for a Douglas fir? Why? she wondered, even as a ribbon of hope began to stream through her insides.

"Uh-huh," she said softly. "And you're bringing me a tree because..."

He unfolded his arms and scraped one palm

across his face as he searched for the words he needed so desperately. "Because I thought the blasted thing could be like a visual aid."

"For what?" She hoped he knew where he was going with this, but Marie wanted to hear him say it.

"To show you that I'm ready for roots."

A bubble of excitement blossomed in her chest. She took a hard grip on it and said, "You are?"

"Yeah." He looked deeply into her eyes and she read so many wonderful things in those familiar blue depths, Marie wanted to shout. But she kept still as he went on. "I want to plant this tree with you and decorate it every year."

"Every year?"

"Yes."

Afraid to believe, afraid not to, Marie stared at him and realized all of her dreams were hanging right there, within reach. "I...don't know what to say," she admitted.

"Don't say anything, Marie," Davis said, and felt his hopes rise as her features softened into the incredibly loving expression he'd missed seeing so much. "Just listen. The last three days I've been a miserable bastard." He paced off a few steps, then walked right back to her. "I've shouted at everyone and made everyone's life hell all because I'm an idiot."

She didn't argue the point. Was that a good sign or a bad one?

He didn't wait to find out. Rushing on with everything he wanted—needed—to tell her, Davis kept talking. "You'd probably be a hell of a lot better off without me, but I'd be in damn poor shape without you."

She smiled. Okay, that was definitely a good sign.

"The last few days without you have been terrible, but they made me realize something. Something I've known all along but was too damn scared to admit."

"What's that, Davis?"

He reached out and laid both hands on her shoulders. Her soft yellow sweater caressed his palms as he looked down into her incredible eyes. "I'm tired of being alone, Marie. I'm tired of pretending it's enough. I want to belong. I want a family." He paused, searched her features for a long moment, then added, "I want *you*."

She didn't say anything. She just blinked at him as her throat knotted.

Say it all, he told himself. Take a risk. Take a chance.

"My enlistment is nearly up," he said, his words tumbling over each other in his hurry to tell her everything he'd been thinking about—planning—the last couple of hours. "I don't want to sign up again. I want to leave the corps and stay here, in Bayside. With you."

Her mouth dropped open. "You do?"

"Yeah," he said on a smile. "I do. I'd like us to expand your shop. Do the restorations we talked about. Be partners. In everything."

"Davis…"

"I know we haven't known each other long, Marie,'' he said quickly, ''but I feel like I've known you forever.''

She reached out and laid one palm on his chest. He accepted it like a benediction, feeling her warmth spiral through him in such a tide of love that he knew he'd never feel the cold again. ''I feel that, too,'' she said softly, and Davis's whole being was swept by relief. He wasn't too late.

His fingers tightened on her shoulders, then he released her and reached into one of his pants pockets for the small, dark blue box he'd brought with him in hope. Opening it up, he held it out to her and said, ''I want to marry you, Marie.''

She looked at the diamond-and-emerald ring for what seemed forever before she lifted her gaze to his again. ''Davis, if this is because you're worried about the possibility of a baby—''

''No!'' He interrupted her quickly, as vehemently as he could. ''No, this is about us. He grabbed her left hand and held it tightly. ''If there is a baby, that's a bonus. What I want—what I *need* is you.''

''Oh, Davis,'' she said on a soft sigh, ''I want to believe you.''

''I love you, Marie.''

She blinked, clearly surprised.

He smiled. ''I'm not afraid to say it anymore. The only thing that scares me is the thought of living without you.''

Marie curled her fingers around his and squeezed. ''You don't have to, Davis. I love you, too.''

He released a pent-up breath and grinned, feeling the power and strength of that smile right down to his soul. "Then you will marry me?" he asked as he took the ring from the box and held it just at her fingertip.

"I will," she said, and he slid the ring home, feeling a sense of satisfaction like nothing he'd ever known before.

Pulling her into his arms, he held her tightly to him, resting his chin on top of her head. Burrowed in close, Marie said, "You know, if you hadn't come here today, I'd already planned on going to the base tomorrow to hunt you down."

He pulled back slightly and smiled down at her. "A recon mission?"

"You bet," she said, and slid her arms around his waist. "And you know the saying... I Always Get My Man."

Davis laughed and shook his head. "That's the mounties, not the marines."

"Who cares?" she asked, going up on her toes.

"Not me, lady," he said and kissed her, promising them both a lifetime of love. And Davis knew the moment his lips touched hers that he had, at long last, found home.

Epilogue

Christmas Eve, afternoon

Davis sat on the floor of Marie's living room, surrounded by what looked to be ten thousand numbered pieces of plastic. And somehow, in the next few hours, he'd have to fit them all together into the space station that Jeremy expected to find beneath the tree tomorrow morning.

"What's the matter, Sarg?" Marie asked from the bedroom doorway. "Giving up already?"

He grinned at her and shook his head. "Marines don't quit."

"Yeah," she said as she walked across the room to him, "but you won't be a marine much longer, will you?"

When she was close enough, he pulled her down onto his lap and gave her a squeeze. "Nope," he said, and didn't feel the least bit sorry about his decision.

One part of his life was over, but a new and even more interesting part was about to begin.

Marie reached up and cupped his cheek. Smoothing her thumb across his skin, she marveled again that they had found each other. She was happier than she'd ever been, and come New Year's Eve, she'd be a bride. And to top that, she had a very special Christmas present for her soon-to-be husband.

"Davis," she said softly, "there's something I want to tell you—"

Footsteps pounding up the stairs outside the apartment interrupted her and they both turned as one when the front door opened and Gina stormed inside. Marie tried to scoot off Davis's lap, but he held her in place.

"What's wrong with you?" Marie asked, settling into the curve of Davis's arms.

"I'm so mad, I could spit," Gina snapped, flashing an angry look at Davis. "This guy in my ballroom dance class? Today he practically dragged me across the floor, and when I told him he was doing everything all wrong, he told me I should just shut up and let the man lead."

"So?" Not that Marie wasn't sympathetic, but she had some plans of her own here.

"*So* I told him that if he had the slightest idea of how to lead, I wouldn't mind at all. And he called me a waste of valuable space." She jammed both fists on her hips and tapped the toe of her shoe against the floor. "Do you believe that? I mean, I'm paying for those lessons. He shouldn't get to insult me like that."

Davis snickered. Marie heard him.

"What do you want us to do about it?" she asked her sister.

"He's a marine, just like *him!*" Gina waved one hand at Davis. "So I figured maybe Davis could have him shot at dawn or something."

"I'll see what I can do," he said. "What's his name? Maybe I know him."

"Nick Peretti," Gina snapped. "He's some kind of sergeant or something."

"Gunnery Sergeant," Davis provided.

"That's it! So you *do* know him." Gina's eyes flashed with sparks of vengeance.

"I've…run into him a time or two," Davis hedged.

"With your car?"

"No."

"Too bad." Then, just as quickly as she'd arrived, Gina turned for the door again. "The next time you see him, you tell him he'd better watch out before ticking off a Santini."

"Oh," Davis said over the slam of the door, "I'll warn him."

In the sudden stillness, Marie shook her head and looked up at him. "Are you absolutely *sure* you want to get involved with this family?"

He laughed.

"I mean it, Davis," she said, one corner of her

mouth curving into a smile, "this is your last chance to retreat."

"Marines don't retreat."

"Good," she said, and leaned into him before giving him his present. "In that case, there's something you should know."

"Yeah?" he asked, reaching past her for section A1 of the space station.

"Gina's going to be an aunt again in about eight months or so."

"That's good...." He stopped dead, slowly turned his head to look down at her, and when he saw her smile, he stammered. "Are—are you sure?"

"I'll see the doctor to be sure. But trust me. We're pregnant." Marie told him, reaching up to touch his face, his mouth.

"Then we're going to have a—"

"Baby."

"Baby," he repeated, awestruck. His right hand drifted to her flat abdomen and rested there lightly, reverently. When he looked at her again, Marie was sure she saw the shimmer of dampness in his eyes, and her heart turned over.

"I love you, Davis," she whispered.

"I love you, Marie."

Then, pulling his head down to hers, she said softly, "Merry Christmas."

Just before his lips found hers, he added. "And a happy new life."

*   *   *   *   *

Silhouette Stars

Born this Month

Monica Seles, Walt Disney, Jeff Bridges, James Galway,
Frank Sinatra, Lee Remick, Keith Richards, Jenny
Agutter, Uri Geller, Mary Tyler Moore

Star of the Month

Sagittarius

A year of progress in many areas of your life,
however, effort will be needed to organise
yourself properly in order to make the best of
what is on offer. Romance is well aspected and
you could find yourself making a commitment
early next year. Take care over finances, read all
the small print before signing contracts.

SILH/HR/0012a

 **Capricorn**

A career move is on the cards but you will need to decide if it is what you want. It could be worth all the disruption that it might cause to your life.

Aquarius

A happy go lucky month with lots of social events on offer. Forget your troubles and catch up on old friends and with opportunities to make new ones too, you should have a ball!

 Pisces

There is the promise of a brighter, happier period in which you may achieve something that's been top of your wish-list for a long while. You could surprise a lot of people, not least yourself!

Aries

The focus is on the home where you will find real happiness and contentment. Old friends make contact and you may be planning an 'out of the ordinary' holiday together.

 Taurus

A busy month with plenty to be done around the home. Enlist the help of those around to make the job quicker and allow you time to relax as well. A touching surprise from a loved one could really lift your spirits.

Gemini

There should be good reason to celebrate this month as the dark clouds lift and you see your life progressing positively. One particular gift brings a wry smile to your face.

Cancer

Listen to your inner soul and act on what you really feel as it could save you from making a big mistake. An old friend re-enters your life late in the month.

Leo

A new opportunity to study, re-train or work in an area that suits you should not be missed. A loved one could pleasantly surprise you mid-month.

Virgo

A great time to start a new project as you should be feeling very creative. A romantic encounter sets your pulse racing, but take care, all may not be as it seems.

Libra

Wipe away the winter blues, take up a new activity, revamp the home. By keeping busy you will feel more positive and your energy will create opportunity.

Scorpio

You should be in a position to make the most of the golden opportunities on offer. Those around you will be happy to support you during this exciting period, so go for it!

© Harlequin Mills & Boon Ltd 2000

**Look out for more
Silhouette Stars next month**

SILHOUETTE DESIRE®

AVAILABLE FROM 22ND DECEMBER 2000

A BRIDE FOR JACKSON POWERS Dixie Browning

Man of the Month

Jackson Powers has only recently discovered he has a baby daughter and sultry stranger Hetty Reynolds is willing to help him find the road to fatherhood. *And* the road to wedded bliss…

THE PRINCESS'S WHITE KNIGHT Carla Cassidy

Royally Wed

A regal princess let loose in the world needed more than a bodyguard—she needed a husband. So royal protector Gabriel Morgan married Princess Serena Wyndham in-name-only. Could this marriage-of-convenience result in a happy-ever-after?

THE DOCTOR WORE SPURS Leanne Banks

Handsome bachelor Dr Tyler Logan always got what he wanted, but when he went to Jill Hershey for fundraising advice he got a lot more than he expected!

MERCENARY'S WOMAN Diana Palmer

Soldiers of Fortune

Sweet Sally Johnson was in danger and Ebenezer Scott fought to protect her. But she yearned for so much more. Could she slip through his defences and become this beloved mercenary's bride?

DID YOU SAY MARRIED?! Kathie DeNosky

Opposites Chance Warren and Kristen Lassiter not only wake up together after a very steamy night, but then find they are married—Vegas-style! Thrown into wedlock, the pair prepare for a baby-on-the-way…

GOING…GOING…WED! Amy J. Fetzer

The Bridal Bid

Bought at a charity auction, Madison Holt was meant to provide domestic help to businessman Alex Donahue. But her innocent kisses had this marriage-shy millionaire dreaming about a different kind of arrangement…

AVAILABLE FROM 22ND DECEMBER 2000

Sensation
Passionate, dramatic, thrilling romances

WILD WAYS Naomi Horton
ANGEL MEETS THE BADMAN Maggie Shayne
THE HARDER THEY FALL Merline Lovelace
ON DANGEROUS GROUND Maggie Price
ON THE WAY TO A WEDDING... Ingrid Weaver
THE PASSION OF PATRICK MACNEILL Virginia Kantra

Intrigue
Danger, deception and suspense

HIS ONLY SON Kelsey Roberts
PROTECTING HIS OWN Molly Rice
HERS TO REMEMBER Karen Lawton Barrett
LITTLE GIRL FOUND Jo Leigh

Special Edition
Vivid, satisfying romances
full of family, life and love

THE COWBOY AND THE NEW YEAR'S BABY
Sherryl Woods
A FAMILY HOMECOMING Laurie Paige
A DOCTOR'S VOW Christine Rimmer
FALLING FOR AN OLDER MAN Trisha Alexander
A COWBOY'S WOMAN Cathy Gillen Thacker
SOUL MATES Carol Finch

FREE

2 BOOKS
AND A SURPRISE GIFT!

We would like to take this opportunity to thank you for reading this Silhouette® book by offering you the chance to take TWO more specially selected titles from the Desire™ series absolutely FREE! We're also making this offer to introduce you to the benefits of the Reader Service™ —

- ★ FREE home delivery
- ★ FREE monthly Newsletter
- ★ FREE gifts and competitions
- ★ Exclusive Reader Service discounts
- ★ Books available before they're in the shops

Accepting these FREE books and gift places you under no obligation to buy; you may cancel at any time, even after receiving your free shipment. Simply complete your details below and return the entire page to the address below. *You don't even need a stamp!*

YES! Please send me 2 free Desire books and a surprise gift. I understand that unless you hear from me, I will receive 4 superb new titles every month for just £2.70 each, postage and packing free. I am under no obligation to purchase any books and may cancel my subscription at any time. The free books and gift will be mine to keep in any case.

D0ZEC

Ms/Mrs/Miss/Mr ....Initials...
BLOCK CAPITALS PLEASE

Surname...

Address...

....

....Postcode ....

Send this whole page to:
UK: FREEPOST CN81, Croydon, CR9 3WZ
EIRE: PO Box 4546, Kilcock, County Kildare (stamp required)

Offer valid in UK and Eire only and not available to current Reader Service subscribers to this series. We reserve the right to refuse an application and applicants must be aged 18 years or over. Only one application per household. Terms and prices subject to change without notice. Offer expires 30th June 2001. As a result of this application, you may receive further offers from Harlequin Mills & Boon Limited and other carefully selected companies. If you would prefer not to share in this opportunity please write to The Data Manager at the address above.

Silhouette® is a registered trademark used under license.
Desire™ is being used as a trademark.